LONGMAN LITERATURE

D1622331

Quartet of Stories

Maya Angelou
Alice Walker
Olive Senior
Lorna Goodison

Editor: Liz Gerschel

LONGMAN

Longman Literature
Series editor: Roy Blatchford

Novels

Jane Austen   *Pride and Prejudice*   0 582 07720 6
Charlotte Brontë   *Jane Eyre*   0 582 07719 2
Emily Brontë   *Wuthering Heights*   0 582 07782 6
Anita Brookner   *Hotel du Lac*   0 582 25406 X
Marjorie Darke   *A Question of Courage*   0 582 25395 0
Charles Dickens   *A Christmas Carol*   0 582 23664 9
                              Great Expectations   0 582 07783 4
                              Hard Times   0 582 25407 8
                              Oliver Twist   0 582 28729 4
George Eliot   *Silas Marner*   0 582 23662 2
Anne Fine   *Flour Babies*   0 582 29259 X
                Goggle-Eyes   0 582 29260 3
                Madame Doubtfire   0 582 29261 1
F Scott Fitzgerald   *The Great Gatsby*   0 582 06023 0
                                 Tender is the Night   0 582 09716 9
Nadine Gordimer   *July's People*   0 582 06011 7
Graham Greene   *The Captain and the Enemy*   0 582 06024 9
Thomas Hardy   *Far from the Madding Crowd*   0 582 07788 5
                         The Mayor of Casterbridge   0 582 22586 8
                         Tess of the d'Urbervilles   0 582 09715 0
Susan Hill   *The Mist in the Mirror*   0 582 25399 3
Aldous Huxley   *Brave New World*   0 582 06016 8
Robin Jenkins   *The Cone-Gatherers*   0 582 06017 6
Doris Lessing   *The Fifth Child*   0 582 06021 4
Joan Lindsay   *Picnic at Hanging Rock*   0 582 08174 2
Bernard Mac Laverty   *Lamb*   0 582 06557 7
Jan Mark   *The Hillingdon Fox*   0 582 25985 1
Dalene Matthee   *Fiela's Child*   0 582 28732 4
Brian Moore   *Lies of Silence*   0 582 08170 X
Beverley Naidoo   *Chain of Fire*   0 582 25403 5
                             Journey to Jo'burg   0 582 25402 7
George Orwell   *Animal Farm*   0 582 06010 9
Alan Paton   *Cry, the Beloved Country*   0 582 07787 7
Ruth Prawer Jhabvala   *Heat and Dust*   0 582 25398 5
Paul Scott   *Staying On*   0 582 07718 4
Virginia Woolf   *To the Lighthouse*   0 582 09714 2

Short stories

Jeffrey Archer   *A Twist in the Tale*   0 582 06022 2
Thomas Hardy   *The Wessex Tales*   0 582 25405 1
Susan Hill   *A Bit of Singing and Dancing*   0 582 09711 8
George Layton   *A Northern Childhood*   0 582 25404 3
Bernard Mac Laverty   *The Bernard Mac Laverty Collection*   0 582 08172 6
Angelou, Goodison, Senior & Walker   *Quartet of Stories*   0 582 28730 8

Poetry

Five Modern Poets   edited by Barbara Bleiman   0 582 09713 4
Poems from Other Centuries   edited by Adrian Tissier   0 582 22595 X
Poems in My Earphone   collected by John Agard   0 582 22587 6
Poems One   edited by Celeste Flower   0 582 25400 0
Poems Two   edited by Paul Jordan & Julia Markus   0 582 25401 9

Other titles in the Longman Literature series are listed on page 164.

Contents

CONTENTS

The writers on writing

Maya Angelou

Maya Angelou was born in 1928 in St Louis, Missouri. When Maya was three, she and her adored brother, Bailey, who was one year older than her, were sent to Stamps, Arkansas, by their mother, to live with their paternal grandmother. She owned a general store, unusual for a black* person in those days in the South, and lived behind it with her other son, Uncle Willie, crippled in a childhood accident.

Maya was happy living with her grandmother, but at seven she and Bailey were taken to live with their mother in California, where her mother's boyfriend raped her. As a result of the shock, Maya stopped talking and remained silent for the next five years, during most of which she lived in Stamps again.

Maya Angelou became a dancer, a singer, an actress, toured Europe and Africa in *Porgy and Bess*, was a waitress, a journalist and an editor, and has been a political activist and Civil Rights campaigner. She lived in Ghana for several years, has married several times and has one son. She has published five volumes of her autobiography: *I Know Why the Caged Bird Sings*, *Gather Together in My Name, Singin' and Swingin' and Gettin' Merry Like Christmas*, *The Heart of a Woman* and *All God's Children Need Travelling*

*Throughout this book the term 'black' is used to refer corporately to people of African descent, whether they are living in Africa, the Caribbean, the United States of America or Britain. Many people who have, in the past, been described as Black Americans, now prefer to describe themselves as African-Americans. Jamaicans call themselves Jamaicans, Caribbean people and, sometimes, West Indians. The term 'black' in this anthology is not used to deny the separate identities of the different peoples of African descent, but as an inclusive term that recognises the many common threads of their experiences in America, the Caribbean and Britain.

Shoes; also several collections of poetry and various film and television scripts. She still acts, sings and directs, and is now Professor of American Studies at Wake Forest University in North Carolina. As she has said, in an interview in **Black Women Writers at Work**, 'you may encounter many defeats but the encountering may be the very experience which creates the vitality and power to endure'.

Maya Angelou's stories in this anthology are taken from **I Know Why the Caged Bird Sings**. She uses her own experience to generalise about how people survived racism and oppression in the South. In selecting events to write about, she chose those that stood out in her mind and rejected those that were too painful or too bad to be written about. She separates writing about her own life from herself as she is, like this:

> It's a strange condition being an autobiographer and a poet. I have to be so internal and yet while writing I have to be apart from the story so that I don't fall into indulgence. Whenever I speak about the books I always think in terms of the Maya character ... I refer to the Maya character so as not to mean me.
>
> Claudia Tate (ed.), **Black Women Writers at Work**
> (Oldcastle Books, 1985)

The important thing about writing is, not to concern oneself too much with 'being an artist', but to get the work done:

> My responsibility as a writer is to be as good as I can be at my craft ... understanding what language can do, gaining control of the language, enables one to make people weep, make them laugh, even make them go to war. You can do this by learning how to harness the power of the word.
>
> **Black Women Writers at Work**

Alice Walker

Alice Walker was born in Eatonton, Georgia, the daughter of a Southern sharecropper, in 1946. She was one of eight children and has written of her childhood in two volumes of essays: *In Search of Our Mothers' Gardens* and *Living by the Word*. It was a hard childhood and, when she was eight, an accident deprived her of sight in one eye. She learnt a great deal from her mother, including her passion for nature.

Alice Walker is conscious of being part of a history – generations of Walkers buried in Eatonton – that ties her to the South. It is her pride that her name links her to one of the bravest of the fighters against slavery, herself an ex-slave, Sojourner Truth, whose famous speech 'Ain't I a woman' was one of the first public statements in the fight to be both black and a woman and free to be who you are. The Greek name 'Alice' means Truth, and her family name, Walker, links her to Sojourner (one who sojourns or travels or walks); in this way she places herself in the ongoing history of black women's search for freedom of expression.

Alice Walker wrote her first stories and poems while she was at university. She began to explore the contradictions between being black and being a feminist, the feminist movement having been largely a white movement. She also began to redefine what is literature. As she said in *In Search of Our Mothers' Gardens*, the writer must 'be her own model as well as the artist, attending, creating, learning from, realising the model, which is to say, herself'. In her collection of essays *In Search of Our Mothers' Gardens* Alice Walker tells the story of her own search for early black women writers. In the essay '**Saving the Life That Is Your Own**' she wrote that, throughout her four years at a prestigious black and then a prestigious white college, she had heard not one word about early black women writers, and that one of her first tasks was simply to determine whether they existed. She has said, 'I think my whole program as a writer is to deal with history just so I know where I am' and that she is writing 'all the things I should have been able to read', to provide herself and other writers with role models to build on.

The stories in this collection are taken from two volumes of her short stories, **You Can't Keep a Good Woman Down** (1971) and **In Love and Trouble** (1973). Alice Walker has published a number of volumes of poetry, short stories and essays, many critical reviews and three novels, including **The Color Purple** which won the Pulitzer Prize in 1983 and was made into a film. She is consulting editor to the political quarterly **Freeways** and to the feminist monthly **Ms**. She has received a number of awards for her writing. She now lives in San Francisco, has a daughter and continues to write and teach about the strength and struggle of black women.

One of the stories by Alice Walker in this collection, '**To Hell with Dying**', is autobiographical; but, she says, the way autobiography works for a writer is different from what you'd think of as being autobiographical. 'None of it actually happened. What happened was the *love* and that is the essence of the story.' By using a basic model from her own life (Mr Sweet did exist and was as she described him) and by inventing a story that would reflect the way she felt about someone she had loved, although the actual events in it had not happened, Alice Walker turned her own experiences into fiction. This technique is one that any writer could try, including the writers who are reading this book.

Olive Senior

Olive Senior was born in 1941, one of ten children of a poor family in a village in Trelawny, a rural and mountainous area of Jamaica. She was sent to live with relatives, who were wealthier and of a higher social class than her own family, in another rural area of Jamaica, Westmoreland. Here she was the only child. The change of family cultures was difficult to accept; she has said that moving between the two households was like 'being shifted between the two extremes of a continuum based on race, colour and class'. Her stories reflect the experience of growing up in rural Jamaican villages, the child's sense of alienation in an adult world, the fear of religion instilled into her in childhood and her feelings about the hypocrisy of some of those attached to the church in Jamaica. The language of the stories captures the oral tradition of storytelling, folk proverbs and biblical sayings which were part of her daily life as a child, as well as the humour of Jamaican Creole.

Olive Senior has a degree from Carleton University, Canada. She has been a journalist and an editor of various cultural and economic journals. She has written an acclaimed reference book on Jamaica *An A–Z of Jamaican Heritage*, various social and political analyses, two collections of poems – *Talking of Trees* and *Gardening in the Tropics* – and three volumes of short stories: *Summer Lightning and other stories*, *Arrival of the snake woman* and *The Discerner of Hearts*. The stories in this anthology have been taken from *Summer Lightning and other stories*, for which she won the Commonwealth Writers' Prize for 1987, the first Caribbean woman to do so.

Olive Senior sees herself as extending the oral tradition in her writing: she captures the vernacular and the folk traditions of Jamaica in her stories, and in her non-fiction writing she records the traditions of the past and the living history of the present. In this way, she says, she is trying to provide a 'memory bank'; to capture the voices and the stories of the oldest generation of Jamaicans and to prevent a heritage being lost or swept away by the tide of influences from Europe and America. Folk stories, duppy (ghost) stories, jokes and storytelling are an essential part of Jamaican life. In her writing, Olive Senior acknowledges the importance of the oral tradition and winds it into a written literature.

Her stories are not autobiographical, but reflect the village life she knew. She has said in an interview, 'Once I have the character fixed in my mind, then I know automatically how the character is going to talk – the words write themselves. I'm very attuned to the sound of the voice. I wouldn't attempt to write the Creole of the street-youth in Kingston: my voices are deep rural. What I'm trying to get across is the voice and how it sounds.'

Lorna Goodison

Lorna Goodison was born in Kingston, Jamaica, one of nine children. She loved growing up in a large family and has said 'we were like a whole country in ourselves'. She studied at the Jamaican School of Art and in New York. Until poetry 'took over' her life, she was primarily an artist and all the covers of her books are taken from her own paintings. She has published three collections of poems – **Tamarind Season**, **I am Becoming My Mother** and **Heartease**, and a collection of short stories, **Baby Mother and the King of Swords**. It is from this collection that the stories in this anthology are taken.

Lorna Goodison has been writer-in-residence at the University of the West Indies and at the Bunting Institute, Radcliffe College, USA, and has held a Fellowship of the University of Iowa. She has won international recognition for her poetry, including the British Airways Commonwealth Poetry Prize (Americas section) in 1986. She has lived in Jamaica, Canada, America and Britain, and has one son, Miles.

Lorna Goodison's stories explore women's experience and, particularly, their relationships with men. Lorna Goodison recognises, in the patterns of relationships between men and women in Jamaica, and even in the way that women of her generation grew up, a heritage of slavery which is still being worked through. In the stories, she identifies the threats and dangers to women's creativity and independence and celebrates the way that Jamaican women empower themselves through what she calls their 'extraordinary womanliness and courage'. Many of her most powerful poems explore her relationship with her mother and with her son. The title of her collection of poems **I am Becoming My Mother** does not simply have the literal meaning of a woman growing more like her own mother as she gets older, but means that in creating her own role model as a writer she is re-creating herself, and thus becoming her own mother.

Like Alice Walker, Lorna Goodison writes the stories she wants to read. Her stories are closely linked to her poetry and explore life in urban and rural Jamaica: the story '**The Dolly Funeral**' is directly autobiographical. Many of the stories draw on her own experiences, especially in the relationships she depicts with men, but they also encapsulate the experiences of other women of her generation. Lorna Goodison recognises, in the way that mothers bring up their daughters 'hard' and in the way that women and men repeat patterns and choices of the past, a hangover from slavery that Jamaica is not yet rid of. She believes that she has been given the power 'to see things that others do not see' and that she must use this spiritual sensitivity.

Her stories have a lyrical, almost incantatory quality (for example, '**I Don't Want to Go Home in the Dark**') but she also has a rich and down-to-earth humour ('**Bella Makes Life**'), because she believes in listening to the voices of her people. She said in a recent interview that she felt that the women characters in her writing wanted her to tell their stories and to speak for the inner strength that motivates them. She shapes these experiences into poetic explorations of women's growth towards self-determination, linked closely to folk culture, the natural world and the spiritual world.

Introduction

History and 'herstory'

The experiences of black peoples, and especially of black women, have largely been invisible in the traditional body of literature in English, or they have been marginalised and presented through the eyes of white writers. There is a black literary tradition – or rather, because of the diaspora (the word used to describe the scattered migration of people across the world), there are a number of black literary traditions – in the Americas, the Caribbean, in Africa and in Britain. Very often the view of the world that black literature presents is a contrast to the world views presented in traditional white literature. In this way, black literature raises questions about the way we see the world, about the language we use and about the cultures that we recognise.

As black women writers are exploring their own experiences, they have had to question the contexts within which they are working as women and as black people. This means they have had to re-examine their history, and look again at their relationships with white men and women, with black men, with their own mothers and fathers and with their children. They have had to see these relationships within the context of societies still affected by racism and sexism and through – for these writers – the English language, the language of white people, of slavery and colonialism, a language that they have had to reshape.

The writers of the stories in this collection have focused on what they know about: their own lives and experiences and the lives of black women before them. They know that they have inherited a shared history: that what their mothers and grandmothers and great-grandmothers experienced has influenced the way they themselves have been brought up, and will exert an influence on the way that they bring up their daughters and their sons. It is a handed-down history that emerges, through the rules that women teach their children for survival and through the stories that mothers tell at the end of the day, or while they are preparing the vegetables or bathing the baby ... 'Did I ever tell you about the time when ...?'

Women's culture has often been described as an oral culture, based on stories, songs and rhymes passed on to children, shared talk between adults, shared laughter, shared tears. The writers of these stories have tried to bring their oral tradition to their writing, to retell their histories, to record the lives of their communities and to share their experiences of life: to make history into *her*story too.

Storytelling and the oral tradition

The short stories in this **Quartet** have been collected under a loose notion of what a short story is: in fact, Maya Angelou's short stories are actually chapters taken from her autobiography. But the writers of the stories in this collection are all poets and story-tellers, weaving into their writing the old oral traditions of their societies: folk culture, proverbs, popular sayings and rhymes, spiritual beliefs and religions, incantations and biblical verses, heard in church or learnt by heart.

The spoken language and the rhythms of voices are reflected in a wide range of language and in storytelling techniques such as repetition, emphasis and onomatopoeia. The oral tradition in literature has often been neglected while attention is focused on the written forms. In this collection the writers draw on the oral traditions of storytelling with which they were all familiar in their childhoods, listening to older people handing on their history – the major events of the shared historical past and their own personal family stories.

Themes in the stories

In these stories the writers have explored issues that are important to them. One of those issues is what is meant by 'love'. The writers have shown love in different social contexts. The struggle for power that often marks relationships between men and women is explored in '**I Don't Want to Go Home in the Dark**', '**The King of Swords**' and '**I Come Through**', but also, more subtly in '**The Boy Who Loved Ice Cream**', and with irony in '**Bella Makes Life**'. The love women give to men is not always sexual: in Alice Walker's '**Nineteen Fifty-Five**', Gracie Mae provides nurture, through her talent as a song-writer and singer, for both her husbands and for Traynor and all those who live off him. And Alice Walker describes an altogether different kind of love in the love of old Mr Sweet in '**To Hell with Dying**'. Love for many women in these stories also means protecting and providing for their children, often while they themselves have to work far away.

The relationships between mothers and children are central to many of these stories although, in some stories, the children are growing up away from their mothers and are being cared for by grandmothers, aunts or other relatives. Grandmother Henderson (in Maya Angelou's writing) provides for and protects Maya and her brother; loving her grandchildren means teaching them to survive in a racist world and protecting them from its effects as far as possible. Maya learns from her what it is to be a strong woman, and what courage having a religious faith can give.

In contrast, the grandparents in '**Love Orange**' have no comprehension of their granddaughter but observe a hollow ritual of child-rearing that reflects meaningless social and religious customs. 'Aunt B' practises 'a strange kind of reverse psychology' on the child in '**The King of Swords**' which is cruel and undermining of her confidence, whereas Auntie Mary and Cherry are teased and manipulated by Beccka, and their hypocrisy contrasts with their show of Christian piety.

The children in these stories do not always understand the adult world, but learn from their experiences. Some, like Myop in '**The Flowers**' or Benjy in '**The Boy Who Loved Ice-Cream**' or the girl in '**Love Orange**' suffer a loss of innocence and learn painfully of the ugliness of the adult world of racism, jealousy and hypocrisy. Others, like Beccka, the young Maya or the girl in '**The Dolly Funeral**', learn to manipulate the adult world, to resist oppression and to survive.

A theme that recurs in many of the stories celebrates women's achievements not only as survivors, but as creators. They are musicians, like Gracie Mae and the singer in '**I Come Through**', or poets, as is the woman in '**I Don't Want to Go Home in the Dark**'. They farm the land, like flowers and live in harmony with nature, recognising 'some things must be left to God', as the poet Robert Frost says in the poem liked best by the woman in '**The King of Swords**'.

Above all, these stories capture the sense of community that permeates women's lives, handing down traditions, teaching daughters and sons how to behave, respecting the old people, uniting and bonding the past and the future. And the women in these stories endure, survive, create, laugh and weep together. Many of the stories are humorous, from the wicked glee of '**Do Angels Wear Brassieres?**' and the comic situations of '**Bella Makes Life**' to the subtle satisfaction of seeing racists get their just deserts in '**Names**' and '**Visit to the Dentist**'. Death and the rites of passage associated with death are explored, the journey from present to future. In these stories women and children learn to shape their own futures, to become powerful and to make their voices heard, while retaining their dignity and integrity.

Historical and political background

Of the four writers in this collection, two are from the Southern states of America and two are from Jamaica. African-American and

Caribbean historical experiences have differed, but there have been common threads, one of which is the legacy of slavery. Slavery was particularly hard on the women, who were heavily outnumbered by the men and were often raped by masters and overseers, and who saw their children sold away from them. It also, of course, had the effect of making some enslaved men feel worthless, unable to protect their women and without responsibility for their children. Many enslaved people found different ways of rebelling against this oppression, but it was not until 1834 that slavery was ended in Jamaica, and not until 1865 was it ended in the whole of the United States.

The position of black people was not immediately much improved after the abolition of slavery in either the USA or Jamaica. The legacy of slavery had a lasting effect on relationships between black and white people. Power was still in the hands of white people and black people were still largely dependent on them. Black people in Jamaica and in the USA began, in different ways, to struggle for power themselves and for the right to determine their own lives. Since 1962 Jamaica has been politically independent of Britain. In the USA, the struggle for equality, particularly in the Southern states, has been long and difficult, from the Civil Rights movement of the 1950s and 1960s to the political debates still going on today.

A note on American spelling

In the stories by Maya Angelou and Alice Walker the authors have used the American English form of spelling, which may seem strange to British readers. Apart from individual words such as *defense* with an 's' or *practice* with a 'c' when used as a verb, there are some spelling patterns which you will come across frequently. The most common of these are 'or' instead of 'our' as in *color*; 'er' instead of 're' as in *center*; the use of a single 'l' in words such as *chiseled* or *chiseling* and 'll' in words like *skillful* and *fulfill*.

Reading Log

The study programme at the back of this book provides many ideas and activities for after you have read the stories. However, you are likely to give a better response to the text if you make some notes as you read. The people who assess your coursework assignments or examination answers are looking for evidence of a personal response to literature; to do well, this should be supported by some close analysis and reference to detail.

Keeping notes as you read should help you to provide this, as well as to keep track of events in the plot, characters and relationships. When you are reading, stop every so often and use the following prompt questions and suggestions to note down key points and details.

Plot

- What have been the main developments in the plot? Note down exactly where they occur.
- How has the author 'moved the story on' – for example, by introducing a new character or by a change of setting?
- Is there more than one storyline?
- How do you expect the plot/s to develop? As you read on, consider whether you predicted accurately or whether there have been some surprises.

Characters

- What are your initial impressions of the main character/s? Are these impressions confirmed or altered as you read? How?

- Do any of the main characters change or develop through the stories? How and why?
- How are you responding to individual characters? In particular, are you aware that you are identifying or sympathising with one of them? Are you conscious of ways in which the author is making or encouraging you to do this, for example by focusing on his/her point of view, or by providing insights into his/her thoughts and feelings?

Setting

The setting of a story is the place (or places) and time in which the events happen. Sometimes the setting involves a particular community or culture. It can often make an important contribution to the prevailing atmosphere of the work.

- How well does the writer help you to visualise the setting? Make a note of any passages of description which you think are particularly effective in creating a vivid sense of place and time.
- Does the setting seem to be just a background against which the action takes place – for example because it is concerned with historical events or with the interrelationship between people and their environment?

Themes

The themes of a work of literature are the *broad* ideas or aspects of experiences which it is about. There are some themes – love, death, war, politics, religion, the environment – which writers have explored throughout the centuries.

- What theme or themes seem to be emerging in each of the stories?

- How is the theme developed? For example, do different characters represent different attitudes or beliefs?
- Does it seem that the writer wants to express her attitude to a theme in order to raise questions, or just to make the reader reflect on it?

Style

- Is the story told by a narrator who is also a character in the stories, referring to herself as 'I' (first person narrative), or is the narrator anonymous and detached from the action (third person narrative)?
- How does this affect the story? For example, does a third-person narrator tell you what characters are thinking and feeling (known as an *omniscient* narrator) or comment directly on characters and/or events?
- Note down any interesting or striking uses of language, such as powerful words and images which evoke a sense of atmosphere. Include any recurring or similar images.
- What do you think of the dialogue? Do the 'voices' of the characters sound real and convincing? Make a note of any particular features of the language used in the dialogue, such as dialect, colloquialisms, slang or expletives (swearing).
- How is the dialogue used – for example to show characters and relationships, for humour, to explore theme?

Your personal response

- How are your feelings about the stories developing as you read? What have you enjoyed or admired most (or least) and why?
- Have the stories made you think about or influenced your views on their themes?

Quartet of Stories

The stories of
Maya Angelou

Incident in the Yard

'Thou shall not be dirty' and 'Thou shall not be impudent' were the two commandments of Grandmother Henderson upon which hung our total salvation.

Each night in the bitterest winter we were forced to wash faces, arms, necks, legs and feet before going to bed. She used to add, with a smirk that unprofane people can't control when venturing into profanity, 'and wash as far as possible, then wash possible.'

We would go to the well and wash in the ice-cold, clear water, grease our legs with the equally cold stiff Vaseline, then tiptoe into the house. We wiped the dust from our toes and settled down for schoolwork, cornbread, clabbered milk, prayers and bed, always in that order. Momma was famous for pulling the quilts off after we had fallen asleep to examine our feet. If they weren't clean enough for her, she took the switch (she kept one behind the bedroom door for emergencies) and woke up the offender with a few aptly placed burning reminders.

The area around the well at night was dark and slick, and boys told about how snakes love water, so that anyone who had to draw water at night and then stand there alone and wash knew that moccasins and rattlers, puff adders and boa constrictors were winding their way to the well and would arrive just as the person washing got soap in her eyes. But Momma convinced us that not only was cleanliness next to Godliness, dirtiness was the inventor of misery.

The impudent child was detested by God and a shame to its parents and could bring destruction to its house and line. All adults had to be addressed as Mister, Missus, Miss, Auntie, Cousin, Unk, Uncle, Buhbah, Sister, Brother and a thousand other appellations indicating familial relationship and the lowliness of the addressor.

Everyone I knew respected these customary laws, except for the powhitetrash children.

Some families of powhitetrash lived on Momma's farm land behind the school. Sometimes a gaggle of them came to the Store, filling the whole room, chasing out the air and even changing the well-known scents. The children crawled over the shelves and into the potato and onion bins, twanging all the time in their sharp voices like cigar-box guitars. They took liberties in my Store that I would never dare. Since Momma told us that the less you say to whitefolks (or even powhite-trash) the better, Bailey and I would stand, solemn, quiet, in the displaced air. But if one of the playful apparitions got close to us, I pinched it. Partly out of angry frustration and partly because I didn't believe in its flesh reality.

They called my uncle by his first name and ordered him around the Store. He, to my crying shame, obeyed them in his limping dip-straight-dip fashion.

My grandmother, too, followed their orders, except that she didn't seem to be servile because she anticipated their needs.

'Here's sugar, Miz Potter, and here's baking powder. You didn't buy soda last month, you'll probably be needing some.'

Momma always directed her statements to the adults, but sometimes, Oh painful sometimes, the grimy, snotty-nosed girls would answer her.

'Naw, Annie...' – to Momma? Who owned the land they lived on? Who forgot more than they would ever learn? If there was any justice in the world, God should strike them dumb at once! – 'Just give us some extry sody crackers, and some more mackerel.'

At least they never looked in her face, or I never caught them doing so. Nobody with a smidgen of training, not even the worst roustabout, would look right in a grown person's face. It meant the person was trying to take the words out before they were formed. The dirty little children didn't do that, but they threw their orders around the Store like lashes from a cat-o'-nine-tails.

When I was around ten years old, those scruffy children caused me the most painful and confusing experience I had ever had with my grandmother.

One summer morning, after I had swept the dirt yard of leaves, spearmint-gum wrappers and Vienna-sausage labels, I raked the yellow-red dirt, and made half-moons carefully, so that the design stood out clearly and mask-like. I put the rake behind the Store and came through the back of the house to find Grandmother on the front porch in her big, wide white apron. The apron was so stiff by virtue of the starch that it could have stood alone. Momma was admiring the yard, so I joined her. It truly looked like a flat redhead that had been raked with a big-toothed comb. Momma didn't say anything but I knew she liked it. She looked over toward the school principal's house and to the right at Mr. McElroy's. She was hoping one of those community pillars would see the design before the day's business wiped it out. Then she looked upward to the school. My head had swung with hers, so at just about the same time we saw a troop of the powhitetrash kids marching over the hill and down by the side of the school.

I looked to Momma for direction. She did an excellent job of sagging from her waist down, but from the waist up she seemed to be pulling for the top of the oak tree across the road. Then she began to moan a hymn. Maybe not to moan, but the tune was so slow and the meter so strange that she could have been moaning. She didn't look at me again. When the children reached halfway down the hill, halfway to the Store, she said without turning, 'Sister, go on inside.'

I wanted to beg her, 'Momma, don't wait for them. Come on inside with me. If they come in the Store, you go to the bedroom and let me wait on them. They only frighten me if you're around. Alone I know how to handle them.' But of course I couldn't say anything, so I went in and stood behind the screen door.

Before the girls got to the porch I heard their laughter crackling and popping like pine logs in a cooking stove. I

6

suppose my lifelong paranoia was born in those cold, molasses-slow minutes. They came finally to stand on the ground in front of Momma. At first they pretended seriousness. Then one of them wrapped her right arm in the crook of her left, pushed out her mouth and started to hum. I realized that she was aping my grandmother. Another said, 'Naw, Helen, you ain't standing like her. This here's it.' Then she lifted her chest, folded her arms and mocked that strange carriage that was Annie Henderson. Another laughed, 'Naw, you can't do it. Your mouth ain't pooched out enough. It's like this.'

I thought about the rifle behind the door, but I knew I'd never be able to hold it straight, and the .410, our sawed-off shotgun, which stayed loaded and was fired every New Year's night, was locked in the trunk and Uncle Willie had the key on his chain. Through the fly-specked screen-door, I could see that the arms of Momma's apron jiggled from the vibrations of her humming. But her knees seemed to have locked as if they would never bend again.

She sang on. No louder than before, but no softer either. No slower or faster.

The dirt of the girls' cotton dresses continued on their legs, feet, arms and faces to make them all of a piece. Their greasy uncolored hair hung down, uncombed, with a grim finality. I knelt to see them better, to remember them for all time. The tears that had slipped down my dress left unsurprising dark spots, and made the front yard blurry and even more unreal. The world had taken a deep breath and was having doubts about continuing to revolve.

The girls had tired of mocking Momma and turned to other means of agitation. One crossed her eyes, stuck her thumbs in both sides of her mouth and said, 'Look here, Annie.' Grandmother hummed on and the apron strings trembled. I wanted to throw a handful of black pepper in their faces, to throw lye on them, to scream that they were dirty, scummy peckerwoods, but I knew I was as clearly imprisoned behind the scene as the actors outside were confined to their roles.

One of the smaller girls did a kind of puppet dance while her fellow clowns laughed at her. But the tall one, who was almost a woman, said something very quietly, which I couldn't hear. They all moved backward from the porch, still watching Momma. For an awful second I thought they were going to throw a rock at Momma, who seemed (except for the apron strings) to have turned into stone herself. But the big girl turned her back, bent down and put her hands flat on the ground – she didn't pick up anything. She simply shifted her weight and did a hand stand.

Her dirty bare feet and long legs went straight for the sky. Her dress fell down around her shoulders, and she had on no drawers. The slick pubic hair made a brown triangle where her legs came together. She hung in the vacuum of that lifeless morning for only a few seconds, then wavered and tumbled. The other girls clapped her on the back and slapped their hands.

Momma changed her song to 'Bread of Heaven, bread of Heaven, feed me till I want no more.'

I found that I was praying too. How long could Momma hold out? What new indignity would they think of to subject her to? Would I be able to stay out of it? What would Momma really like me to do?

Then they were moving out of the yard, on their way to town. They bobbed their heads and shook their slack behinds and turned, one at a time:

''Bye, Annie.'

''Bye, Annie.'

''Bye, Annie.'

Momma never turned her head or unfolded her arms, but she stopped singing and said, ''Bye, Miz Helen, 'bye, Miz Ruth, 'bye, Miz Eloise.'

I burst. A firecracker July-the-Fourth burst. How could Momma call them Miz? The mean nasty things. Why couldn't she have come inside the sweet, cool store when we saw them breasting the hill? What did she prove? And then if they were dirty, mean and impudent, why did Momma have to call them Miz?

She stood another whole song through and then opened the screen door to look down on me crying in rage. She looked until I looked up. Her face was a brown moon that shone on me. She was beautiful. Something had happened out there, which I couldn't completely understand, but I could see that she was happy. Then she bent down and touched me as mothers of the church 'lay hands on the sick and afflicted' and I quieted.

'Go wash your face, Sister.' And she went behind the candy counter and hummed, 'Glory, glory, hallelujah, when I lay my burden down.'

I threw the well water on my face and used the weekday handkerchief to blow my nose. Whatever the contest had been out front, I knew Momma had won.

I took the rake back to the front yard. The smudged footprints were easy to erase. I worked for a long time on my new design and laid the rake behind the wash pot. When I came back in the Store, I took Momma's hand and we both walked outside to look at the pattern.

It was a large heart with lots of hearts growing smaller inside, and piercing from the outside rim to the smallest heart was an arrow. Momma said, 'Sister, that's right pretty.' Then she turned back to the Store and resumed, 'Glory, glory, hallelujah, when I lay my burden down.'

Names

Recently a white woman from Texas, who would quickly describe herself as a liberal, asked me about my home-town. When I told her that in Stamps my grandmother had owned the only Negro general merchandise store since the turn of the century, she exclaimed, 'Why, you were a debutante.' Ridiculous and even ludicrous. But Negro girls in small Southern towns, whether poverty-stricken or just munching along on a few of life's necessities, were given as extensive and irrelevant preparations for adulthood as rich white girls shown in magazines. Admittedly the training was not the same. While white girls learned to waltz and sit gracefully with a tea cup balanced on their knees, we were lagging behind, learning the mid-Victorian values with very little money to indulge them. (Come and see Edna Lomax spending the money she made picking cotton on five balls of ecru tatting thread. Her fingers are bound to snag the work and she'll have to repeat the stitches time and time again. But she knows that when she buys the thread.)

We were required to embroider and I had trunkfuls of colorful dishtowels, pillowcases, runners and handkerchiefs to my credit. I mastered the art of crocheting and tatting, and there was a lifetime's supply of dainty doilies that would never be used in sacheted dresser drawers. It went without saying that all girls could iron and wash, but the finer touches around the home, like setting a table with real silver, baking roasts and cooking vegetables without meat, had to be learned elsewhere. Usually at the source of those habits. During my tenth year, a white woman's kitchen became my finishing school.

Mrs. Viola Cullinan was a plump woman who lived in a three-bedroom house somewhere behind the post office. She was singularly unattractive until she smiled, and then the lines around her eyes and mouth which made her look perpetually dirty disappeared, and her face looked like the mask of an impish elf. She usually rested her smile until late afternoon when her women friends dropped in and Miss Glory, the cook, served them cold drinks on the closed-in porch.

The exactness of her house was inhuman. This glass went here and only here. That cup had its place and it was an act of impudent rebellion to place it anywhere else. At twelve o'clock the table was set. At 12:15 Mrs. Cullinan sat down to dinner (whether her husband had arrived or not). At 12:16 Miss Glory brought out the food.

It took me a week to learn the difference between a salad plate, a bread plate and a dessert plate.

Mrs. Cullinan kept up the tradition of her wealthy parents. She was from Virginia. Miss Glory, who was a descendant of slaves that had worked for the Cullinans, told me her history. She had married beneath her (according to Miss Glory). Her husband's family hadn't had their money very long and what they had 'didn't 'mount to much'.

As ugly as she was, I thought privately, she was lucky to get a husband above or beneath her station. But Miss Glory wouldn't let me say a thing against her mistress. She was very patient with me, however, over the housework. She explained the dishware, silverware and servants' bells. The large round bowl in which soup was served wasn't a soup bowl, it was a tureen. There were goblets, sherbet glasses, ice-cream glasses, wine glasses, green glass coffee cups with matching saucers, and water glasses. I had a glass to drink from, and it sat with Miss Glory's on a separate shelf from the others. Soup spoons, gravy boat, butter knives, salad forks and carving platter were additions to my vocabulary and in fact almost represented a new language. I was fascinated with the novelty, with the fluttering Mrs. Cullinan and her Alice-in-Wonderland house.

Her husband remains, in my memory, undefined. I lumped him with all the other white men that I had ever seen and tried not to see.

On our way home one evening, Miss Glory told me that Mrs. Cullinan couldn't have children. She said that she was too delicate-boned. It was hard to imagine bones at all under those layers of fat. Miss Glory went on to say that the doctor had taken out all her lady organs. I reasoned that a pig's organs included the lungs, heart and liver, so if Mrs. Cullinan was walking around without those essentials, it explained why she drank alcohol out of unmarked bottles. She was keeping herself embalmed.

When I spoke to Bailey about it, he agreed that I was right, but he also informed me that Mr. Cullinan had two daughters by a colored lady and that I knew them very well. He added that the girls were the spitting image of their father. I was unable to remember what he looked like, although I had just left him a few hours before, but I thought of the Coleman girls. They were very light-skinned and certainly didn't look very much like their mother (no one ever mentioned Mr. Coleman).

My pity for Mrs. Cullinan preceded me the next morning like the Cheshire cat's smile. Those girls, who could have been her daughters, were beautiful. They didn't have to straighten their hair. Even when they were caught in the rain, their braids still hung down straight like tamed snakes. Their mouths were pouty little cupid's bows. Mrs. Cullinan didn't know what she missed. Or maybe she did. Poor Mrs. Cullinan.

For weeks after, I arrived early, left late and tried very hard to make up for her barrenness. If she had had her own children, she wouldn't have had to ask me to run a thousand errands from her back door to the back door of her friends. Poor old Mrs. Cullinan.

Then one evening Miss Glory told me to serve the ladies on the porch. After I set the tray down and turned toward the kitchen, one of the women asked, 'What's your name, girl?' It was the speckled-faced one. Mrs. Cullinan said, 'She doesn't talk much. Her name's Margaret.'

'Is she dumb?'

'No. As I understand it, she can talk when she wants to but she's usually quiet as a little mouse. Aren't you, Margaret?'

I smiled at her. Poor thing. No organs and couldn't even pronounce my name correctly.

'She's a sweet little thing, though.'

'Well, that may be, but the name's too long. I'd never bother myself. I'd call her Mary if I was you.'

I fumed into the kitchen. That horrible woman would never have the chance to call me Mary because if I was starving I'd never work for her. I decided I wouldn't pee on her if her heart was on fire. Giggles drifted in off the porch and into Miss Glory's pots. I wondered what they could be laughing about.

Whitefolks were so strange. Could they be talking about me? Everybody knew that they stuck together better than the Negroes did. It was possible that Mrs. Cullinan had friends in St. Louis who heard about a girl from Stamps being in court and wrote to tell her. Maybe she knew about Mr. Freeman.

My lunch was in my mouth a second time and I went outside and relieved myself on the bed of four-o'clocks. Miss Glory thought I might be coming down with something and told me to go on home, that Momma would give me some herb tea, and she'd explain to her mistress.

I realized how foolish I was being before I reached the pond. Of course Mrs. Cullinan didn't know. Otherwise she wouldn't have given me the two nice dresses that Momma cut down, and she certainly wouldn't have called me a 'sweet little thing'. My stomach felt fine, and I didn't mention anything to Momma.

That evening I decided to write a poem on being white, fat, old and without children. It was going to be a tragic ballad. I would have to watch her carefully to capture the essence of her loneliness and pain.

The very next day, she called me by the wrong name. Miss Glory and I were washing up the lunch dishes when Mrs. Cullinan came to the doorway. 'Mary?'

Miss Glory asked, 'Who?'

Mrs. Cullinan, sagging a little, knew and I knew. 'I want Mary to go down to Mrs. Randall's and take her some soup. She's not been feeling well for a few days.'

Miss Glory's face was a wonder to see. 'You mean Margaret, ma'am. Her name's Margaret.'

'That's too long. She's Mary from now on. Heat that soup from last night and put it in the china tureen and, Mary, I want you to carry it carefully.'

Every person I knew had a hellish horror of being 'called out of his name'. It was a dangerous practice to call a Negro anything that could be loosely construed as insulting because of the centuries of their having been called niggers, jigs, dinges, blackbirds, crows, boots and spooks.

Miss Glory had a fleeting second of feeling sorry for me. Then as she handed me the hot tureen she said, 'Don't mind, don't pay that no mind. Sticks and stones may break your bones, but words... You know, I been working for her for twenty years.'

She held the back door open for me. 'Twenty years. I wasn't much older than you. My name used to be Hallelujah. That's what Ma named me, but my mistress give me 'Glory', and it stuck. I likes it better too.'

I was in the little path that ran behind the houses when Miss Glory shouted, 'It's shorter too.'

For a few seconds it was a tossup over whether I would laugh (imagine being named Hallelujah) or cry (imagine letting some white woman rename you for her convenience). My anger saved me from either outburst. I had to quit the job, but the problem was going to be how to do it. Momma wouldn't allow me to quit for just any reason.

'She's a peach. That woman is a real peach.' Mrs. Randall's maid was talking as she took the soup from me, and I wondered what her name used to be and what she answered to now.

For a week I looked into Mrs. Cullinan's face as she called me Mary. She ignored my coming late and leaving early. Miss

Glory was a little annoyed because I had begun to leave egg yolk on the dishes and wasn't putting much heart in polishing the silver. I hoped that she would complain to our boss, but she didn't.

Then Bailey solved my dilemma. He had me describe the contents of the cupboard and the particular plates she liked best. Her favorite piece was a casserole shaped like a fish and the green glass coffee cups. I kept his instructions in mind, so on the next day when Miss Glory was hanging out clothes and I had again been told to serve the old biddies on the porch, I dropped the empty serving tray. When I heard Mrs. Cullinan scream, 'Mary!' I picked up the casserole and two of the green glass cups in readiness. As she rounded the kitchen door I let them fall on the tiled floor.

I could never absolutely describe to Bailey what happened next, because each time I got to the part where she fell on the floor and screwed up her ugly face to cry, we burst out laughing. She actually wobbled around on the floor and picked up shards of the cups and cried, 'Oh, Momma. Oh, dear Gawd. It's Momma's china from Virginia. Oh, Momma, I sorry.'

Miss Glory came running in from the yard and the women from the porch crowded around. Miss Glory was almost as broken up as her mistress. 'You mean to say she broke our Virginia dishes? What we gone do?'

Mrs. Cullinan cried louder, 'That clumsy nigger. Clumsy little black nigger.'

Old speckled-face leaned down and asked, 'Who did it, Viola? Was it Mary? Who did it?'

Everything was happening so fast I can't remember whether her action preceded her words, but I know that Mrs. Cullinan said, 'Her name's Margaret, goddamn it, her name's Margaret.' And she threw a wedge of the broken plate at me. It could have been the hysteria which put her aim off, but the flying crockery caught Miss Glory right over her ear and she started screaming.

15

I left the front door wide open so all the neighbors could hear.

Mrs. Cullinan was right about one thing. My name wasn't Mary.

Visit to the Dentist

The Angel of the candy counter had found me out at last, and was exacting excruciating penance for all the stolen Milky Ways, Mounds, Mr. Goodbars and Hersheys with Almonds. I had two cavities that were rotten to the gums. The pain was beyond the bailiwick of crushed aspirins or oil of cloves. Only one thing could help me, so I prayed earnestly that I'd be allowed to sit under the house and have the building collapse on my left jaw. Since there was no Negro dentist in Stamps, nor doctor either, for that matter, Momma had dealt with previous toothaches by pulling them out (a string tied to the tooth with the other end looped over her fist), pain killers and prayer. In this particular instance the medicine had proved ineffective; there wasn't enough enamel left to hook a string on, and the prayers were being ignored because the Balancing Angel was blocking their passage.

I lived a few days and nights in blinding pain, not so much toying with as seriously considering the idea of jumping in the well, and Momma decided I had to be taken to a dentist. The nearest Negro dentist was in Texarkana, twenty-five miles away, and I was certain that I'd be dead long before we reached half the distance. Momma said we'd go to Dr. Lincoln, right in Stamps, and he'd take care of me. She said he owed her a favor.

I knew there were a number of whitefolks in town that owed her favors. Bailey and I had seen the books which showed how she had lent money to Blacks and whites alike during the Depression, and most still owed her. But I couldn't aptly remember seeing Dr. Lincoln's name, nor had I ever heard of a Negro's going to him as a patient. However, Momma said we were going, and put water on the stove for our baths. I had never been to a doctor, so she told me that after the bath (which would make my mouth feel better) I had to put on freshly starched and ironed underclothes from inside out. The

17

ache failed to respond to the bath, and I knew then that the pain was more serious than that which anyone had ever suffered.

Before we left the Store, she ordered me to brush my teeth and then wash my mouth with Listerine. The idea of even opening my clamped jaws increased the pain, but upon her explanation that when you go to a doctor you have to clean yourself all over, but most especially the part that's to be examined, I screwed up my courage and unlocked my teeth. The cool air in my mouth and the jarring of my molars dislodged what little remained of my reason. I had frozen to the pain, my family nearly had to tie me down to take the toothbrush away. It was no small effort to get me started on the road to the dentist. Momma spoke to all the passers-by, but didn't stop to chat. She explained over her shoulder that we were going to the doctor and she'd 'pass the time of day' on our way home.

Until we reached the pond the pain was my world, an aura that haloed me for three feet around. Crossing the bridge into whitefolks' country, pieces of sanity pushed themselves forward. I had to stop moaning and start walking straight. The white towel, which was drawn under my chin and tied over my head, had to be arranged. If one was dying, it had to be done in style if the dying took place in whitefolks' part of town.

On the other side of the bridge the ache seemed to lessen as if a whitebreeze blew off the whitefolks and cushioned everything in their neighborhood – including my jaw. The gravel road was smoother, the stones smaller and the tree branches hung down around the path and nearly covered us. If the pain didn't diminish then, the familiar yet strange sights hypnotized me into believing that it had.

But my head continued to throb with the measured insistence of a bass drum, and how could a toothache pass the calaboose, hear the songs of the prisoners, their blues and laughter, and not be changed? How could one or two or even a mouthful of angry tooth roots meet a wagonload of powhitetrash children, endure their idiotic snobbery and not feel less important?

Behind the building which housed the dentist's office ran a small path used by servants and those tradespeople who catered to the butcher and Stamps' one restaurant. Momma and I followed that lane to the backstairs of Dentist Lincoln's office. The sun was bright and gave the day a hard reality as we climbed up the steps to the second floor.

Momma knocked on the back door and a young white girl opened it to show surprise at seeing us there. Momma said she wanted to see Dentist Lincoln and to tell him Annie was there. The girl closed the door firmly. Now the humiliation of hearing Momma describe herself as if she had no last name to the young white girl was equal to the physical pain. It seemed terribly unfair to have a toothache and a headache and have to bear at the same time the heavy burden of Blackness.

It was always possible that the teeth would quiet down and maybe drop out of their own accord. Momma said we would wait. We leaned in the harsh sunlight on the shaky railings of the dentist's back porch for over an hour.

He opened the door and looked at Momma. 'Well, Annie, what can I do for you?'

He didn't see the towel around my jaw or notice my swollen face.

Momma said, 'Dentist Lincoln. It's my grandbaby here. She got two rotten teeth that's giving her a fit.'

She waited for him to acknowledge the truth of her statement. He made no comment, orally or facially.

'She had this toothache purt' near four days now, and today I said, "Young lady, you going to the Dentist."'

'Annie?'

'Yes, sir, Dentist Lincoln.'

He was choosing words the way people hunt for shells. 'Annie, you know I don't treat nigra, colored people.'

'I know, Dentist Lincoln. But this here is just my little grandbaby, and she ain't gone be no trouble to you...'

'Annie, everybody has a policy. In this world you have

19

to have a policy. Now, my policy is I don't treat colored people.'

The sun had baked the oil out of Momma's skin and melted the Vaseline in her hair. She shone greasily as she leaned out of the dentist's shadow.

'Seem like to me, Dentist Lincoln, you might look after her, she ain't nothing but a little mite. And seems like maybe you owe me a favor or two.'

He reddened slightly. 'Favor or no favor. The money has all been repaid to you and that's the end of it. Sorry, Annie.' He had his hand on the doorknob. 'Sorry.' His voice was a bit kinder on the second 'Sorry,' as if he really was.

Momma said, 'I wouldn't press on you like this for myself but I can't take No. Not for my grandbaby. When you come to borrow my money you didn't have to beg. You asked me, and I lent it. Now, it wasn't my policy. I ain't no moneylender, but you stood to lose this building and I tried to help you out.'

'It's been paid, and raising your voice won't make me change my mind. My policy...' He let go of the door and stepped nearer Momma. The three of us were crowded on the small landing. 'Annie, my policy is I'd rather stick my hand in a dog's mouth than in a nigger's.'

He had never once looked at me. He turned his back and went through the door into the cool beyond. Momma backed up inside herself for a few minutes. I forgot everything except her face which was almost a new one to me. She leaned over and took the doorknob, and in her everyday soft voice she said, 'Sister, go on downstairs. Wait for me. I'll be there directly.'

Under the most common of circumstances I knew it did no good to argue with Momma. So I walked down the steep stairs, afraid to look back and afraid not to do so. I turned as the door slammed, and she was gone.

Momma walked in that room as if she owned it. She shoved that silly nurse aside with one hand and strode into the dentist's office. He was sitting in his chair, sharpening his mean instruments and putting extra sting into his medicines. Her eyes were blazing like live coals and her arms had doubled themselves in length. He looked up at her just before she caught him by the collar of his white jacket.

'Stand up when you see a lady, you contemptuous scoundrel.' Her tongue had thinned and the words rolled off well enunciated. Enunciated and sharp like little claps of thunder.

The dentist had no choice but to stand at R.O.T.C. attention. His head dropped after a minute and his voice was humble. 'Yes, ma'am, Mrs. Henderson.'

'You knave, do you think you acted like a gentleman, speaking to me like that in front of my granddaughter?' She didn't shake him, although she had the power. She simply held him upright.

'No, ma'am, Mrs. Henderson.'

'No, ma'am, Mrs. Henderson, what?' Then she did give him the tiniest of shakes, but because of her strength the action set his head and arms to shaking loose on the ends of his body. He stuttered much worse than Uncle Willie. 'No, ma'am, Mrs. Henderson, I'm sorry.'

With just an edge of her disgust showing, Momma slung him back in his dentist's chair. 'Sorry is as sorry does, and you're about the sorriest dentist I ever laid my eyes on.' (She could afford to slip into the vernacular because she had such eloquent command of English.)

'I didn't ask you to apologize in front of Marguerite, because I don't want her to know my power, but I order you, now and herewith. Leave Stamps by sundown.'

'Mrs. Henderson, I can't get my equipment...' He was shaking terribly now.

'Now, that brings me to my second order. You will never again practice dentistry. Never! When you get settled in your next place, you will be a vegetarian caring for dogs with the mange, cats with the cholera and cows with the epizootic. Is that clear?'

The saliva ran down his chin and his eyes filled with tears. 'Yes, ma'am. Thank you for not killing me. Thank you, Mrs. Henderson.'

Momma pulled herself back from being ten feet tall with eight-foot arms and said, 'You're welcome for nothing, you varlet, I wouldn't waste a killing on the likes of you.'

On her way out she waved her handkerchief at the nurse and turned her into a crocus sack of chicken feed.

Momma looked tired when she came down the stairs, but who wouldn't be tired if they had gone through what she had. She came close to me and adjusted the towel under my jaw (I had forgotten the toothache; I only knew that she made her hands gentle in order not to awaken the pain). She took my hand. Her voice never changed. 'Come on, Sister.'

I reckoned we were going home where she would concoct a brew to eliminate the pain and maybe give me new teeth too. New teeth that would grow overnight out of my gums. She led me toward the drugstore, which was in the opposite direction from the Store. 'I'm taking you to Dentist Baker in Texarkana.'

I was glad after all that that I had bathed and put on Mum and Cashmere Bouquet talcum powder. It was a wonderful surprise. My toothache had quieted to solemn pain, Momma had obliterated the evil white man, and we were going on a trip to Texarkana, just the two of us.

On the Greyhound she took an inside seat in the back, and I sat beside her. I was so proud of being her granddaughter and sure that some of her magic must have come down to me. She asked if I was scared. I only shook my head and leaned over on her cool brown upper arm. There was no chance that a dentist, especially a Negro dentist, would dare hurt me then. Not with Momma there. The trip was uneventful, except that she put her arm around me, which was very unusual for Momma to do.

The dentist showed me the medicine and the needle before he deadened my gums, but if he hadn't I wouldn't have worried. Momma stood right behind him. Her arms were folded and she checked on everything he did. The teeth were extracted and she bought me an ice cream cone from the side window of a drug counter. The trip back to Stamps was quiet, except that I had to spit into a very small empty snuff can which she had gotten for me and it was difficult with the bus humping and jerking on our country roads.

At home, I was given a warm salt solution, and when I washed out my mouth I showed Bailey the empty holes, where the clotted blood sat like filling in a pie crust. He said I was quite brave, and that was my cue to reveal our confrontation with the peckerwood dentist and Momma's incredible powers.

I had to admit that I didn't hear the conversation, but what else could she have said than what I said she said? What else done? He agreed with my analysis in a lukewarm way, and I happily (after all, I'd been sick) flounced into the Store. Momma was preparing our evening meal and Uncle Willie leaned on the door sill. She gave her version.

'Dentist Lincoln got right uppity. Said he'd rather put his hand in a dog's mouth. And when I reminded him of the favor, he brushed it off like a piece of lint. Well, I sent Sister downstairs and went inside. I hadn't never been in his office before, but I found the door to where he takes out teeth, and him and the nurse was in there thick as thieves. I just stood there till he caught sight of me.' Crash bang the pots on the stove. 'He jumped just like he was sitting on a pin. He said, "Annie, I done tole you, I ain't gonna mess around in no niggah's mouth." I said, "Somebody's got to do it then," and he said, "Take her to Texarkana to the colored dentist" and that's when I said, "If you paid me my money I could afford to take her." He said, "It's all been paid." I tole him everything but the interest been paid. He said "'Twasn't no interest." I said "'Tis now, I'll take ten dollars as payment in full." You know, Willie, it wasn't no right thing to do, 'cause I lent that money without thinking about it.

'He tole that little snippity nurse of his'n to give me ten dollars and make me sign a 'paid in full' receipt. She gave it to me and I signed the papers. Even though by rights he was paid up before, I figger, he gonna be that kind of nasty, he gonna have to pay for it.'

Momma and her son laughed and laughed over the white man's evilness and her retributive sin.

I preferred, much preferred, my version.

The stories of
Alice Walker

Nineteen Fifty-Five

1955

The car is a brandnew red Thunderbird convertible, and it's
passed the house more than once. It slows down real slow now,
and stops at the curb. An older gentleman dressed like a
Baptist deacon gets out on the side near the house, and a
young fellow who looks about sixteen gets out on the driver's
side. They are white, and I wonder what in the world they
doing in this neighborhood.

Well, I say to J.T., put your shirt on, anyway, and let me
clean these glasses offa the table.

We had been watching the ballgame on TV. I wasn't
actually watching, I was sort of daydreaming, with my foots up
in J.T.'s lap.

I seen 'em coming on up the walk, brisk, like they coming to
sell something, and then they rung the bell, and J.T. declined
to put on a shirt but instead disappeared into the bedroom
where the other television is. I turned down the one in the
living room; I figured I'd be rid of these two double quick and
J.T. could come back out again.

Are you Gracie Mae Still? asked the old guy, when I opened
the door and put my hand on the lock inside the screen.

And I don't need to buy a thing, said I.

What makes you think we're sellin'? he asks, in that hearty
Southern way that makes my eyeballs ache.

Well, one way or another and they're inside the house
and the first thing the young fellow does is raise the TV a
couple of decibels. He's about five feet nine, sort of womanish
looking, with real dark white skin and a red pouting mouth.
His hair is black and curly and he looks like a Loosianna
creole.

About one of your songs, says the deacon. He is maybe sixty,
with white hair and beard, white silk shirt, black linen suit,

black tie and black shoes. His cold gray eyes look like they're sweating.

One of my songs?

Traynor here just *loves* your songs. Don't you, Traynor? He nudges Traynor with his elbow. Traynor blinks, says something I can't catch in a pitch I don't register.

The boy learned to sing and dance livin' round you people out in the country. Practically cut his teeth on you.

Traynor looks up at me and bites his thumbnail.

I laugh.

Well, one way or another they leave with my agreement that they can record one of my songs. The deacon writes me a check for five hundred dollars, the boy grunts his awareness of the transaction, and I am laughing all over myself by the time I rejoin J. T.

Just as I am snuggling down beside him though I hear the front door bell going off again.

Forgit his hat? asks J. T.

I hope not, I say.

The deacon stands there leaning on the door frame and once again I'm thinking of those sweaty-looking eyeballs of his. I wonder if sweat makes your eyeballs pink because his are sure pink. Pink and gray and it strikes me that nobody I'd care to know is behind them.

I forgot one little thing, he says pleasantly. I forgot to tell you Traynor and I would like to buy up all of those records you made of the song. I tell you we sure do love it.

Well, love it or not, I'm not so stupid as to let them do that without making 'em pay. So I says, Well, that's gonna cost you. Because, really, that song never did sell all that good, so I was glad they was going to buy it up. But on the other hand, them two listening to my song by themselves, and nobody else getting to hear me sing it, give me a pause.

Well, one way or another the deacon showed me where I would come out ahead on any deal he had proposed so far. Didn't I give you five hundred dollars? he asked. What white man – and don't even need to mention colored – would give you more? We buy up all your records of that particular song: first, you git royalties. Let me ask you, how much you sell that song for in the first place? Fifty dollars? A hundred, I say. And no royalties from it yet, right? Right. Well, when we buy up all of them records you gonna git royalties. And that's gonna make all them race record shops sit up and take notice of Gracie Mae Still. And they gonna push all them other records of yourn they got. And you no doubt will become one of the big name colored recording artists. And then we can offer you another five hundred dollars for letting us do all this for you. And by God you'll be sittin' pretty! You can go out and buy you the kind of outfit a star should have. Plenty sequins and yards of red satin.

I had done unlocked the screen when I saw I could get some more money out of him. Now I held it wide open while he squeezed through the opening between me and the door. He whipped out another piece of paper and I signed it.

He sort of trotted out to the car and slid in beside Traynor, whose head was back against the seat. They swung around in a u-turn in front of the house and then they was gone.

J. T. was putting his shirt on when I got back to the bedroom. Yankees beat the Orioles 10–6, he said. I believe I'll drive out to Paschal's pond and go fishing. Wanta go?

While I was putting on my pants. J. T. was holding the two checks.

I'm real proud of a woman that can make cash money without leavin' home, he said. And I said *Umph*. Because we met on the road with me singing in first one little low-life jook after another, making ten dollars a night for myself if I was lucky, and sometimes bringin' home nothing but my life. And J. T. just loved them times. The way I was fast and flashy and always on the go from one town to another. He loved the way my singin' made the dirt farmers cry like babies and the womens shout Honey, hush! But that's mens. They loves any style to which you can get 'em accustomed.

28

1956

My little grandbaby called me one night on the phone: Little Mama, Little Mama, there's a white man on the television singing one of your songs! Turn on channel 5.

Lord, if it wasn't Traynor. Still looking half asleep from the neck up, but kind of awake in a nasty way from the waist down. He wasn't doing too bad with my song either, but it wasn't just the song the people in the audience was screeching and screaming over, it was that nasty little jerk he was doing from the waist down.

Well, Lord have mercy, I said, listening to him. If I'da closed my eyes, it could have been me. He had followed every turning of my voice, side streets, avenues, red lights, train crossings and all. It give me a chill.

Everywhere I went I heard Traynor singing my song, and all the little white girls just eating it up. I never had so many ponytails switched across my line of vision in my life. They was so *proud*. He was a *genius*.

Well, all that year I was trying to lose weight anyway and that and high blood pressure and sugar kept me pretty well occupied. Traynor had made a smash from a song of mine, I still had seven hundred dollars of the original one thousand dollars in the bank, and I felt if I could just bring my weight down, life would be sweet.

1957

I lost ten pounds in 1956. That's what I give myself for Christmas. And J. T. and me and the children and their friends and grandkids of all description had just finished dinner – over which I had put on nine and a half of my lost ten – when who should appear at the front door but Traynor. Little Mama, Little Mama! It's that white man who sings — — —. The children didn't call it my song anymore. Nobody did. It was funny how that happened. Traynor and the deacon had bought up all my records, true, but on his record he had put 'written

29

by Gracie Mae Still.' But that was just another name on the label, like 'produced by Apex Records'.

On the TV he was inclined to dress like the deacon told him. But now he looked presentable.

Merry Christmas, said he.

And same to you, Son.

I don't know why I called him Son. Well, one way or another they're all our sons. The only requirement is that they be younger than us. But then again, Traynor seemed to be aging by the minute.

You looks tired, I said. Come on in and have a glass of Christmas cheer.

J. T. ain't never in his life been able to act decent to a white man he wasn't working for, but he poured Traynor a glass of bourbon and water, then he took all the children and grandkids and friends and whatnot out to the den. After while I heard Traynor's voice singing the song, coming from the stereo console. It was just the kind of Christmas present my kids would consider cute.

I looked at Traynor, complicit. But he looked like it was the last thing in the world he wanted to hear. His head was pitched forward over his lap, his hands holding his glass and his elbows on his knees.

I done sung that song seem like a million times this year, he said. I sung it on the Grand Ole Opry, I sung it on the Ed Sullivan show. I sung it on Mike Douglas, I sung it at the Cotton Bowl, the Orange Bowl. I sung it at Festivals. I sung it at Fairs. I sung it overseas in Rome, Italy, and once in a submarine *underseas*. I've sung it and sung it, and I'm making forty thousand dollars a day offa it, and you know what, I don't have the faintest notion what that song means.

Whatchumean, what do it mean? It mean what it says. All I could think was: These suckers is making forty thousand a *day* offa my song and now they gonna come back and try to swindle me out of the original thousand.

It's just a song, I said. Cagey. When you fool around with a

30

lot of no count mens you sing a bunch of 'em. I shrugged.

Oh, he said. Well. He started brightening up. I just come by to tell you I think you are a great singer.

He didn't blush, saying that. Just said it straight out.

And I brought you a little Christmas present too. Now you take this little box and you hold it until I drive off. Then you take it outside under that first streetlight back up the street aways in front of that green house. Then you open the box and see... Well, just *see*.

What had come over this boy, I wondered, holding the box. I looked out the window in time to see another white man come up and get in the car with him and then two more cars full of white mens start out behind him. They was all in long black cars that looked like a funeral procession.

Little Mama, Little Mama, what it is? One of my grandkids come running up and started pulling at the box. It was wrapped in gay Christmas paper – the thick, rich kind that it's hard to picture folks making just to throw away.

J. T. and the rest of the crowd followed me out the house, up the street to the streetlight and in front of the green house. Nothing was there but somebody's gold-grilled white Cadillac. Brandnew and most distracting. We got to looking at it so till I almost forgot the little box in my hand. While the others were busy making 'miration I carefully took off the paper and ribbon and folded them up and put them in my pants pocket. What should I see but a pair of genuine solid gold caddy keys.

Dangling the keys in front of everybody's nose, I unlocked the caddy, motioned for J. T. to git in on the other side, and us didn't come back home for two days.

1960
Well, the boy was sure nuff famous by now. He was still a mite shy of twenty but already they was calling him the Emperor of Rock and Roll.

Then what should happen but the draft.

31

Well, says J.T. There goes all this Emperor of Rock and Roll business.

But even in the army the womens was on him like white on rice. We watched it on the News.

Dear Gracie Mae [he wrote from Germany],

How you? Fine I hope as this leaves me doing real well. Before I come in the army I was gaining a lot of weight and gitting jittery from making all them dumb movies. But now I exercise and eat right and get plenty of rest. I'm more awake than I been in ten years.

I wonder if you are writing any more songs?

Sincerely,
Traynor

I wrote him back:

Dear Son,

We is all fine in the Lord's good grace and hope this finds you the same. J.T. and me be out all times of the day and night in that car you give me – which you know you didn't have to do. Oh, and I do appreciate the mink and the new self-cleaning oven. But if you send anymore stuff to eat from Germany I'm going to have to open up a store in the neighborhood just to get rid of it. Really, we have more than enough of everything. The Lord is good to us and we don't know Want.

Glad to here you is well and gitting your right rest. There ain't nothing like exercising to help that along. J.T. and me work some part of every day that we don't go fishing in the garden.

Well, so long Soldier.

Sincerely,
Gracie Mae

He wrote:

Dear Gracie Mae,

I hope you and J.T. like that automatic power tiller I had one of the stores back home send you. I went through a mountain of catalogs looking for it – I wanted something that even a woman could use.

I've been thinking about writing some songs of my own but every time I finish one it don't seem to be about nothing I've actually lived myself. My agent keeps sending me other people's songs but they just sound mooney. I can hardly git through 'em without gagging.

Everybody still loves that song of yours. They ask me all the time what do I think it means, really. I mean, they want to know just what I want to know. Where out of your life did it come from?

Sincerely,
Traynor

1968

I didn't see the boy for seven years. No. Eight. Because just about everybody was dead when I saw him again. Malcolm X, King, the president and his brother, and even J. T. J. T. died of a head cold. It just settled in his head like a block of ice, he said, and nothing we did moved it until one day he just leaned out the bed and died.

His good friend Horace helped me put him away, and then about a year later Horace and me started going together. We was sitting out on the front porch swing one summer night, dusk-dark, and I saw this great procession of lights winding to a stop.

Holy Toledo! said Horace. (He's got a real sexy voice like Ray Charles.) Look *at* it. He meant the long line of flashy cars and the white men in white summer suits jumping out on the drivers' sides and standing at attention. With wings they could pass for angels, with hoods they could be the Klan.

Traynor comes waddling up the walk.

And suddenly I know what it is he could pass for. An Arab like the ones you see in storybooks. Plump and soft and with never a care about weight. Because with so much money, who cares? Traynor is almost dressed like someone from a storybook too. He has on, I swear, about ten necklaces. Two sets of bracelets on his arms, at least one ring on every finger, and

33

some kind of shining buckles on his shoes, so that when he walks you get quite a few twinkling lights.

Gracie Mae, he says, coming up to give me a hug. J. T.

I explain that J. T. passed. That this is Horace.

Horace, he says, puzzled but polite, sort of rocking back on his heels, Horace.

That's it for Horace. He goes in the house and don't come back.

Looks like you and me is gained a few, I say.

He laughs. The first time I ever heard him laugh. It don't sound much like a laugh and I can't swear that it's better than no laugh a'tall.

He's gitting fat for sure, but he's still slim compared to me. I'll never see three hundred pounds again and I've just about said (excuse me) f☆☆☆ it. I got to thinking about it one day an' I thought: aside from the fact that they say it's unhealthy, my fat ain't never been no trouble. Mens always have loved me. My kids ain't never complained. Plus they's fat. And fat like I is I looks distinguished. You see me coming and know somebody's *there*.

Gracie Mae, he says, I've come with a personal invitation to you to my house tomorrow for dinner. He laughed. What did it sound like? I couldn't place it. See them men out there? he asked me. I'm sick and tired of eating with them. They don't never have nothing to talk about. That's why I eat so much. But if you come to dinner tomorrow we can talk about the old days. You can tell me about that farm I bought you.

I sold it, I said.

You did?

Yeah, I said, I did. Just cause I said I liked to exercise by working in a garden didn't mean I wanted five hundred acres! Anyhow, I'm a city girl now. Raised in the country it's true. Dirt poor – the whole bit – but that's all behind me now.

Oh well, he said, I didn't mean to offend you.

We sat a few minutes listening to the crickets.

Then he said: You wrote that song while you was still on the farm, didn't you, or was it right after you left?

You had somebody spying on me? I asked.

You and Bessie Smith got into a fight over it once, he said.

You *is* been spying on me!

But I don't know what the fight was about, he said. Just like I don't know what happened to your second husband. Your first one died in the Texas electric chair. Did you know that? Your third one beat you up, stole your touring costumes and your car and retired with a chorine to Tuskegee. He laughed. He's still there.

I had been mad, but suddenly I calmed down. Traynor was talking very dreamily. It was dark but seems like I could tell his eyes weren't right. It was like some*thing* was sitting there talking to me but not necessarily with a person behind it.

You gave up on marrying and seem happier for it. He laughed again. I married but it never went like it was supposed to. I never could squeeze any of my own life either into it or out of it. It was like singing somebody else's record. I copied the way it was sposed to be *exactly* but I never had a clue what marriage meant.

I bought her a diamond ring big as your fist. I bought her clothes. I built her a mansion. But right away she didn't want the boys to stay there. Said they smoked up the bottom floor. Hell, there were *five* floors.

No need to grieve, I said. No need to. Plenty more where she come from.

He perked up. That's part of what that song means, ain't it? No need to grieve. Whatever it is, there's plenty more down the line.

I never really believed that way back when I wrote that song, I said. It was all bluffing then. The trick is to live long enough to put your young bluffs to use. Now if I was to sing that song today I'd tear it up. 'Cause I done lived long enough to know it's *true*. Them words could hold me up.

I ain't lived that long, he said.

35

Look like you on your way, I said. I don't know why, but the boy seemed to need some encouraging. And I don't know, seem like one way or another you talk to rich white folks and you end up reassuring *them*. But what the hell, by now I feel something for the boy. I wouldn't be in his bed all alone in the middle of the night for nothing. Couldn't be nothing worse than being famous the world over for something you don't even understand. That's what I tried to tell Bessie. She wanted that same song. Overheard me practicing it one day, said, with her hands on her hips: Gracie Mae, I'ma sing your song tonight. I *likes* it.

Your lips be too swole to sing, I said. She was mean and she was strong, but I trounced her.

Ain't you famous enough with your own stuff? I said. Leave mine alone. Later on, she thanked me. By then she was Miss Bessie Smith to the World, and I was still Miss Gracie Mae Nobody from Notasulga.

The next day all these limousines arrived to pick me up. Five cars and twelve bodyguards. Horace picked that morning to start painting the kitchen.

Don't paint the kitchen, fool, I said. The only reason that dumb boy of ours is going to show me his mansion is because he intends to present us with a new house.

What you gonna do with it? he asked me, standing there in his shirtsleeves stirring the paint.

Sell it. Give it to the children. Live in it on weekends. It don't matter what I do. He sure don't care.

Horace just stood there shaking his head. Mama you sure looks *good*, he says. Wake me up when you git back.

Fool, I say, and pat my wig in front of the mirror.

The boy's house is something else. First you come to this mountain, and then you commence to drive and drive up this road that's lined with magnolias. Do magnolias grow on mountains? I was wondering. And you come to lakes and you come to ponds and you come to deer and you come up on some sheep. And I figure these two is sposed to represent England and Wales. Or something out of Europe. And you just keep on coming to stuff. And it's all pretty. Only the man driving my car don't look at nothing but the road. Fool. And then *finally*, after all this time, you begin to go up the driveway. And there's more magnolias – only they're not in such good shape. It's sort of cool up this high and I don't think they're gonna make it. And then I see this building that looks like if it had a name it would be The Tara Hotel. Columns and steps and outdoor chandeliers and rocking chairs. Rocking chairs? Well, and there's the boy on the steps dressed in a dark green satin jacket like you see folks wearing on TV late at night, and he looks sort of like a fat dracula with all that house rising behind him, and standing beside him there's this little white vision of loveliness that he introduces as his wife.

He's nervous when he introduces us and he says to her: This is Gracie Mae Still, I want you to know me. I mean . . . and she gives him a look that would fry meat.

Won't you come in, Gracie Mae, she says, and that's the last I see of her.

He fishes around for something to say or do and decides to escort me to the kitchen. We go through the entry and the parlor and the breakfast room and the dining room and the servants' passage and finally get there. The first thing I notice is that, altogether, there are five stoves. He looks about to introduce me to one.

Wait a minute, I say. Kitchens don't do nothing for me. Let's go sit on the front porch.

Well, we hike back and we sit in the rocking chairs rocking until dinner.

Gracie Mae, he says down the table, taking a piece of fried chicken from the woman standing over him, I got a little surprise for you.

It's a house, ain't it? I ask, spearing a chitlin.

You're getting *spoiled*, he says. And the way he says *spoiled* sounds funny. He slurs it. It sounds like his tongue is too thick for his mouth. Just that quick he's finished the chicken and is now eating chitlins *and* a pork chop. *Me* spoiled, I'm thinking.

I already got a house. Horace is right this minute painting the kitchen. I bought that house. My kids feel comfortable in that house.

But this one I bought you is just like mine. Only a little smaller.

I still don't need no house. And anyway who would clean it?

He looks surprised.

Really, I think, some peoples advance *so* slowly.

I hadn't thought of that. But what the hell, I'll get you somebody to live in.

I don't want other folks living 'round me. Makes me nervous.

You *don't?* It *do?*

What I want to wake up and see folks I don't even know for?

He just sits there downtable staring at me. Some of that feeling is in the song, ain't it? Not the words, the *feeling*. What I want to wake up and see folks I don't even know for? But I see twenty folks a day I don't even know, including my wife.

This food wouldn't be bad to wake up to though, I said. The boy had found the genius of corn bread.

He looked at me real hard. He laughed. Short. They want what you got but they don't want you. They want what I got only it ain't mine. That's what makes 'em so hungry for me when I sing. They getting the flavor of something but they ain't getting the thing itself. They like a pack of hound dogs trying to gobble up a scent.

You talking 'bout your fans?

Right. Right. He says.

Don't worry 'bout your fans, I say. They don't know their asses from a hole in the ground. I doubt there's a honest one in the bunch.

That's the point. Dammit, that's the point! He hits the table with his fist. It's so solid it don't even quiver. You need a honest audience! You can't have folks that's just gonna lie right back to you.

Yeah, I say, it was small compared to yours, but I had one. It would have been worth my life to try to sing 'em somebody else's stuff that I didn't know nothing about.

He must have pressed a buzzer under the table. One of his flunkies zombies up.

Git Johnny Carson, he says.

On the phone? asks the zombie.

On the phone, says Traynor, what you think I mean, git him offa the front porch? Move your ass.

So two weeks later we's on the Johnny Carson show.

Traynor is all corseted down nice and looks a little bit fat but mostly good. And all the women that grew up on him and my song squeal and squeal. Traynor says: The lady who wrote my first hit record is here with us tonight, and she's agreed to sing it for all of us, just like she sung it forty-five years ago. Ladies and Gentlemen, the great Gracie Mae Still!

Well, I had tried to lose a couple of pounds my own self, but failing that I had me a very big dress made. So I sort of rolls over next to Traynor, who is dwarfted by me, so that when he puts his arm around back of me to try to hug me it looks funny to the audience and they laugh.

I can see this pisses him off. But I smile out there at 'em. Imagine squealing for twenty years and not knowing why you're squealing? No more sense of endings and beginnings than hogs.

It don't matter, Son, I say. Don't fret none over me.

I commence to sing. And I sound — wonderful. Being able to sing good ain't all about having a good singing voice a'tall. A good singing voice helps. But when you come up in the Hard Shell Baptist church like I did you understand early that the fellow that sings is the singer. Them that waits for programs and arrangements and letters from home is just good voices occupying body space.

So there I am singing my own song, my own way. And I give it all I got and enjoy every minute of it. When I finish Traynor is standing up clapping and clapping and beaming at first me and then the audience like I'm his mama for true. The audience claps politely for about two seconds.

Traynor looks disgusted.

He comes over and tries to hug me again. The audience laughs.

Johnny Carson looks at us like we both weird.

Traynor is mad as hell. He's supposed to sing something called a love ballad. But instead he takes the mike, turns to me and says: Now see if my imitation still holds up. He goes into the same song, *our* song, I think, looking out at his flaky audience. And he sings it just the way he always did. My voice, my tone, my inflection, everything. But he forgets a couple of lines. Even before he's finished the matronly squeals begin.

He sits down next to me looking whipped.

It don't matter, Son, I say, patting his hand. You don't even know those people. Try to make the people you know happy.

Is that in the song? he asks.

Maybe. I say.

1977

For a few years I hear from him, then nothing. But trying to lose weight takes all the attention I got to spare. I finally faced up to the fact that my fat is the hurt I don't admit, not even to myself, and that I been trying to bury it from the day I was born. But also when you git real old, to tell the truth, it ain't as pleasant. It gits lumpy and slack. Yuck. So one day I said to Horace, I'ma git this shit offa me.

And he fell in with the program like he always try to do and Lord such a procession of salads and cottage cheese and fruit juice!

One night I dreamed Traynor had split up with his fifteenth wife. He said: *You meet 'em for no reason. You date 'em for no reason. You marry 'em for no reason. I do it all but I swear it's just like somebody else doing it. I feel like I can't remember Life.*

The boy's in trouble, I said to Horace.

You've always said that, he said.

I have?

Yeah. You always said he looked asleep. You can't sleep through life if you wants to live it.

You not such a fool after all, I said, pushing myself up with my cane and hobbling over to where he was. Let me sit down on your lap, I said, while this salad I ate takes effect.

In the morning we heard Traynor was dead. Some said fat, some said heart, some said alcohol, some said drugs. One of the children called from Detroit. Them dumb fans of his is on a crying rampage, she said. You just ought to turn on the TV.

But I didn't want to see 'em. They was crying and crying and didn't even know what they was crying for. One day this is going to be a pitiful country, I thought.

The Flowers

It seemed to Myop as she skipped lightly from hen house to pigpen to smokehouse that the days had never been as beautiful as these. The air held a keenness that made her nose twitch. The harvesting of the corn and cotton, peanuts and squash, made each day a golden surprise that caused excited little tremors to run up her jaws.

Myop carried a short, knobby stick. She struck out at random at chickens she liked, and worked out the beat of a song on the fence around the pigpen. She felt light and good in the warm sun. She was ten, and nothing existed for her but her song, the stick clutched in her dark brown hand, and the tat-de-ta-ta-ta of accompaniment.

Turning her back on the rusty boards of her family's sharecropper cabin, Myop walked along the fence till it ran into the stream made by the spring. Around the spring, where the family got drinking water, silver ferns and wild-flowers grew. Along the shallow banks pigs rooted. Myop watched the tiny white bubbles disrupt the thin black scale of soil and the water that silently rose and slid away down the stream.

She had explored the woods behind the house many times. Often, in late autumn, her mother took her to gather nuts among the fallen leaves. Today she made her own path, bouncing this way and that way, vaguely keeping an eye out for snakes. She found, in addition to various common but pretty ferns and leaves, an armful of strange blue flowers with velvety ridges and a sweetsuds bush full of the brown, fragrant buds.

By twelve o'clock, her arms laden with sprigs of her findings, she was a mile or more from home. She had often been as far before, but the strangeness of the land made it not as pleasant as her usual haunts. It seemed gloomy in the little cove in which she found herself. The air was damp, the silence close and deep.

Myop began to circle back to the house, back to the peacefulness of the morning. It was then she stepped smack into his eyes. Her heel became lodged in the broken ridge between brow and nose, and she reached down quickly, unafraid, to free herself. It was only when she saw his naked grin that she gavé a little yelp of surprise.

He had been a tall man. From feet to neck covered a long space. His head lay beside him. When she pushed back the leaves and layers of earth and debris Myop saw that he'd had large white teeth, all of them cracked or broken, long fingers, and very big bones. All his clothes had rotted away except some threads of blue denim from his overalls. The buckles of the overalls had turned green.

Myop gazed around the spot with interest. Very near where she'd stepped into the head was a wild pink rose. As she picked it to add to her bundle she noticed a raised mound, a ring, around the rose's root. It was the rotted remains of a noose, a bit of shredding plowline, now blending benignly into the soil. Around an overhanging limb of a great spreading oak clung another piece. Frayed, rotted, bleached, and frazzled – barely there – but spinning restlessly in the breeze. Myop laid down her flowers.

And the summer was over.

To Hell with Dying

'To hell with dying,' my father would say. 'These children want Mr. Sweet!'

Mr. Sweet was a diabetic and an alcoholic and a guitar player and lived down the road from us on a neglected cotton farm. My older brothers and sisters got the most benefit from Mr. Sweet, for when they were growing up he had quite a few years ahead of him and so was capable of being called back from the brink of death any number of times – whenever the voice of my father reached him as he lay expiring. 'To hell with dying, man,' my father would say, pushing the wife away from the bedside (in tears although she knew the death was not necessarily the last one unless Mr. Sweet really wanted it to be). 'These children want Mr. Sweet!' And they did want him, for at a signal from Father they would come crowding around the bed and throw themselves on the covers, and whoever was the smallest at the time would kiss him all over his wrinkled brown face and begin to tickle him so that he would laugh all down in his stomach, and his moustache, which was long and sort of straggly, would shake like Spanish moss and was also that color.

Mr. Sweet had been ambitious as a boy, wanted to be a doctor or lawyer or sailor, only to find that black men fare better if they are not. Since he could become none of these things he turned to fishing as his only earnest career and playing the guitar as his only claim to doing anything extraordinarily well. His son, the only one that he and his wife, Miss Mary, had, was shiftless as the day is long and spent money as if he were trying to see the bottom of the mint, which Mr. Sweet would tell him was the clean brown palm of his hand. Miss Mary loved her 'baby', however, and worked hard to get him the 'li'l necessaries' of life, which turned out mostly to be women.

Mr. Sweet was a tall, thinnish man with thick kinky hair going dead white. He was dark brown, his eyes were very squinty and sort of bluish, and he chewed Brown Mule tobacco. He was constantly on the verge of being blind drunk, for he brewed his own liquor and was not in the least a stingy sort of man, and was always very melancholy and sad, though frequently when he was 'feelin' good' he'd dance around the yard with us, usually keeling over just as my mother came to see what the commotion was.

Toward all of us children he was very kind, and had the grace to be shy with us, which is unusual in grownups. He had great respect for my mother for she never held his drunkenness against him and would let us play with him even when he was about to fall in the fireplace from drink. Although Mr. Sweet would sometimes lose complete or nearly complete control of his head and neck so that he would loll in his chair, his mind remained strangely acute and his speech not too affected. His ability to be drunk and sober at the same time made him an ideal playmate, for he was as weak as we were and we could usually best him in wrestling, all the while keeping a fairly coherent conversation going.

We never felt anything of Mr. Sweet's age when we played with him. We loved his wrinkles and would draw some on our brows to be like him, and his white hair was my special treasure and he knew it and would never come to visit us just after he had had his hair cut off at the barbershop. Once he came to our house for something, probably to see my father about fertilizer for his crops because, although he never paid the slightest attention to his crops, he liked to know what things would be best to use on them if he ever did. Anyhow, he had not come with his hair since he had just had it shaved off at the barbershop. He wore a huge straw hat to keep off the sun and also to keep his head away from me. But as soon as I saw him I ran up and demanded that he take me up and kiss me with his funny beard which smelled so strongly of tobacco. Looking forward to burying my small fingers into his woolly hair I threw away his hat only to find he had done something to his hair, that it was no longer there! I let out a squall which made my mother think that Mr. Sweet had finally dropped me in the well or something and from that day I've been wary of men in hats. However, not long after, Mr. Sweet showed up with his hair grown out and just as white and kinky and impenetrable as it ever was.

Mr. Sweet used to call me his princess, and I believed it. He made me feel pretty at five and six, and simply outrageously devastating at the blazing age of eight and a half. When he came to our house with his guitar the whole family would stop whatever they were doing to sit around him and listen to him play. He liked to play 'Sweet Georgia Brown', that was what he called me sometimes, and also he liked to play 'Caldonia' and all sorts of sweet, sad, wonderful songs which he sometimes made up. It was from one of these songs that I learned that he had had to marry Miss Mary when he had in fact loved somebody else (now living in Chi-ca-go, or De-stroy, Michigan). He was not sure that Joe Lee, her 'baby', was also his baby. Sometimes he would cry and that was an indication that he was about to die again. And so we would all get prepared, for we were sure to be called upon.

I was seven the first time I remember actually participating in one of Mr. Sweet's 'revivals' – my parents told me I had participated before, I had been the one chosen to kiss him and tickle him long before I knew the rite of Mr. Sweet's rehabilitation. He had come to our house, it was a few years after his wife's death, and was very sad, and also, typically, very drunk. He sat on the floor next to me and my older brother, the rest of the children were grown up and lived elsewhere, and began to play his guitar and cry. I held his woolly head in my arms and wished I could have been old enough to have been the woman he loved so much and that I had not been lost years and years ago.

When he was leaving, my mother said to us that we'd better sleep light that night for we'd probably have to go over to Mr.

Sweet's before daylight. And we did. For soon after we had gone to bed one of the neighbors knocked on our door and called my father and said that Mr. Sweet was sinking fast and if he wanted to get in a word before the crossover he'd better shake a leg and get over to Mr. Sweet's house. All the neighbors knew to come to our house if something was wrong with Mr. Sweet, but they did not know how we always managed to make him well, or at least stop him from dying, when he was often so near death. As soon as we heard the cry we got up, my brother and I and my mother and father, and put on our clothes. We hurried out of the house and down the road for we were always afraid that we might someday be too late and Mr. Sweet would get tired of dallying.

When we got to the house, a very poor shack really, we found the front room full of neighbors and relatives and someone met us at the door and said that it was all very sad that old Mr. Sweet Little (for Little was his family name, although we mostly ignored it) was about to kick the bucket. My parents were advised not to take my brother and me into the 'death room', seeing we were so young and all, but we were so much more accustomed to the death room than he that we ignored him and dashed in without giving his warning a second thought. I was almost in tears, for these deaths upset me fearfully, and the thought of how much depended on me and my brother (who was such a ham most of the time) made me very nervous.

The doctor was bending over the bed and turned back to tell us for at least the tenth time in the history of my family that, alas, old Mr. Sweet Little was dying and that the children had best not see the face of implacable death (I didn't know what 'implacable' was, but whatever it was, Mr. Sweet was not!). My father pushed him rather abruptly out of the way saying, as he always did and very loudly for he was saying it to Mr. Sweet, 'To hell with dying, man, these children want Mr. Sweet' – which was my cue to throw myself upon the bed and kiss Mr. Sweet all around the whiskers and under the eyes and around the collar of his nightshirt where he smelled so strongly of all sorts of things, mostly liniment.

I was very good at bringing him around, for as soon as I saw that he was struggling to open his eyes I knew he was going to be all right, and so could finish my revival sure of success. As soon as his eyes were open he would begin to smile and that way I knew that I had surely won. Once, though, I got a tremendous scare, for he could not open his eyes and later I learned that he had had a stroke and that one side of his face was stiff and hard to get into motion. When he began to smile I could tickle him in earnest because I was sure that nothing would get in the way of his laughter, although once he began to cough so hard that he almost threw me off his stomach, but that was when I was very small, little more than a baby, and my bushy hair had gotten in his nose.

When we were sure he would listen to us we would ask him why he was in bed and when he was coming to see us again and could we play with his guitar, which more than likely would be leaning against the bed. His eyes would get all misty and he would sometimes cry out loud, but we never let it embarrass us, for he knew that we loved him and that we sometimes cried too for no reason. My parents would leave the room to just the three of us; Mr. Sweet, by that time, would be propped up in bed with a number of pillows behind his head and with me sitting and lying on his shoulder and along his chest. Even when he had trouble breathing he would not ask me to get down. Looking into my eyes he would shake his white head and run a scratchy old finger all around my hairline, which was rather low down, nearly to my eyebrows, and made some people say I looked like a baby monkey.

My brother was very generous in all this, he let me do all the revivaling – he had done it for years before I was born and so was glad to be able to pass it on to someone new. What he would do while I talked to Mr. Sweet was pretend to play the guitar, in fact pretend that he was a young version of Mr. Sweet, and it always made Mr. Sweet glad to think that someone wanted to be like him – of course, we did not know this then, we played the thing by ear, and whatever he seemed to like, we did. We were desperately afraid that he was just going to take off one day and leave us.

It did not occur to us that we were doing anything special; we had not learned that death was final when it did come. We thought nothing of triumphing over it so many times, and in fact became a trifle contemptuous of people who let themselves be carried away. It did not occur to us that if our own father had been dying we could not have stopped it, that Mr. Sweet was the only person over whom we had power.

When Mr. Sweet was in his eighties I was studying in the university many miles from home. I saw him whenever I went home, but he was never on the verge of dying that I could tell and I began to feel that my anxiety for his health and psychological well-being was unnecessary. By this time he not only had a moustache but a long flowing snow-white beard, which I loved and combed and braided for hours. He was very peaceful, fragile, gentle, and the only jarring note about him was his old steel guitar, which he still played in the old sad, sweet, down-home blues way.

On Mr. Sweet's ninetieth birthday I was finishing my doctorate in Massachusetts and had been making arrangements to go home for several weeks' rest. That morning I got a telegram telling me that Mr. Sweet was dying again and could I please drop everything and come home. Of course I could. My dissertation could wait and my teachers would understand when I explained to them when I got back. I ran to the phone, called the airport, and within four hours I was speeding along the dusty road to Mr. Sweet's.

The house was more dilapidated than when I was last there, barely a shack, but it was overgrown with yellow roses which my family had planted many years ago. The air was heavy and sweet and very peaceful. I felt strange walking through the gate and up the old rickety steps. But the strangeness left me as I caught sight of the long white beard I loved so well

49

flowing down the thin body over the familiar quilt coverlet. Mr. Sweet!

His eyes were closed tight and his hands, crossed over his stomach, were thin and delicate, no longer scratchy. I remembered how always before I had run and jumped up on him just anywhere; now I knew he would not be able to support my weight. I looked around at my parents, and was surprised to see that my father and mother also looked old and frail. My father, his own hair very gray, leaned over the quietly sleeping old man, who, incidentally, smelled still of wine and tobacco, and said, as he'd done so many times, 'To hell with dying, man! My daughter is home to see Mr. Sweet!' My brother had not been able to come as he was in the war in Asia. I bent down and gently stroked the closed eyes and gradually they began to open. The closed, wine-stained lips twitched a little, then parted in a warm slightly embarrassed smile. Mr. Sweet could see me and he recognized me and his eyes looked very spry and twinkly for a moment. I put my head down on the pillow next to his and we just looked at each other for a long time. Then he began to trace my peculiar hairline with a thin, smooth finger. I closed my eyes when his finger halted above my ear (he used to rejoice at the dirt in my ears when I was little), his hand stayed cupped around my cheek. When I opened my eyes, sure that I had reached him in time, his were closed.

Even at twenty-four how could I believe that I had failed? that Mr. Sweet was really gone? He had never gone before. But when I looked up at my parents I saw that they were holding back tears. They had loved him dearly. He was like a piece of rare and delicate china which was always being saved from breaking and which finally fell. I looked long at the old face, the wrinkled forehead, the red lips, the hands that still reached out to me. Soon I felt my father pushing something cool into my hands. It was Mr. Sweet's guitar. He had asked them months before to give it to me; he had known that even if I came next time he would not be able to respond in the old way. He did not want me to feel that my trip had been for nothing.

The old guitar! I plucked the strings, hummed 'Sweet Georgia Brown'. The magic of Mr. Sweet lingered still in the cool steel box. Through the window I could catch the fragrant delicate scent of tender yellow roses. The man on the high old-fashioned bed with the quilt coverlet and the flowing white beard had been my first love.

The stories of
Olive Senior

Love Orange

Work out your own salvation with fear and trembling.

Phillipians

Somewhere between the repetition of Sunday School lessons and the broken doll which the lady sent me one Christmas I lost what it was to be happy. But I didn't know it then even though in dreams I would lie with my face broken like the doll's in the pink tissue of a shoebox coffin. For I was at the age where no one asked me for commitment and I had a phrase which I used like a talisman. When strangers came or lightning flashed, I would lie in the dust under my grand-father's vast bed and hug the dog, whispering 'our worlds wait outside' and be happy.

Once I set out to find the worlds outside, the horizon was wide and the rim of the far mountains beckoned. I was happy when they found me in time for bed and a warm supper, for the skies, I discovered, were the same shade of China blue as the one intact eye of the doll. 'Experience can wait,' I whispered to the dog, 'death too.'

I knew all about death then because in dreams I had been there. I also knew a great deal about love. Love, I thought, was like an orange, a fixed and sharply defined amount, limited, finite. Each person had this amount of love to distribute as he may. If one had many people to love then the segments for each person would be smaller and eventually love, like patience, would be exhausted. That is why I preferred to live with my grandparents then since they had fewer people to love than my parents and so my portion of their love-orange would be larger.

My own love-orange I jealously guarded. Whenever I thought of love I could feel it in my hand, large and round and brightly coloured, intact and spotless. I had moments of indecision when I wanted to distribute the orange but each time I would grow afraid of the audacity of such commitment. Sometimes, in a moment of rare passion, I would extend the orange to the dog or my grandmother but would quickly withdraw my hand each time. For without looking I would feel in its place the doll crawling into my hand and nestling there and I would run into the garden and be sick. I would see its face as it lay in the pink tissue of a shoebox tied with ribbons beside the stocking hanging on the bedpost and I would clutch my orange tighter, thinking that I had better save it for the day when occasions like this would arise again and I would need the entire orange to overcome the feelings which arose each time I thought of the doll.

I could not let my grandmother know about my being sick because she never understood about the doll. For years I had dreamed of exchanging homemade dolls with button eyes and ink faces for a plaster doll with blue eyes and limbs that moved. All that December I haunted my grandmother's clothes closet until beneath the dresses I discovered the box smelling faintly of camphor and without looking I knew that it came from Miss Evangeline's toy shop and that it would therefore be a marvel. But the doll beside the Christmas stocking, huge in a billowing dress and petticoats, had half a face and a finger missing. 'It can be mended,' my grandmother said, 'I can make it as good as new. "Why throw away a good thing?" Miss Evangeline said as she gave it to me.'

But I could no longer hear I could no longer see for the one China blue eye and the missing finger that obscured my vision. And after that I never opened a box again and I never waited up for Christmas. And although I buried the box beneath the allamanda tree the doll rose up again and again, in my throat, like a sickness to be got rid of from the body, and I felt as if I too were half a person who could lay down in the shoebox and sleep forever. But on awakening from these moments, I would find safely clutched in my hands the orange, conjured up from some deep part of myself, and I would hug the dog saying 'our worlds wait outside'.

That summer I saw more clearly the worlds that awaited. It was filled with many deaths that seemed to tie all the strands of my life together and which bore some oblique relationship to both the orange and the doll.

The first to die was a friend of my grandparents who lived nearby. I sometimes played with her grandchildren at her house when I was allowed to, but each time she had appeared only as a phantom, come on the scene silently, her feet shod in cotton stockings rolled down to her ankles, thrust into a pair of her son's broken down slippers. In all the years I had known her I had never heard her say anything but whisper softly; her whole presence was a whisper. She seemed to appear from the cracks of the house, the ceiling, anywhere, she made so little noise in her coming, this tiny, delicate, slightly absurd old woman who lived for us only in the secret and mysterious prison of the aged.

When she died it meant nothing to me, I could think then only of my death which I saw nightly in dreams but I could not conceive of her in the flesh, to miss her or to weep tears.

The funeral that afternoon was 5.00 p.m. on a hot summer's day. My grandmother dressed me all in white and I trailed down the road behind her, my corseted and whaleboned grandmother lumbering from side to side in a black romaine dress now shiny in the sunlight, bobbing over her head a huge black umbrella. My grandfather stepped high in shiny black shoes and a shiny black suit ahead of her. Bringing up the rear, I skipped lightly on the gravel, clutching in my hand a new, shiny, bright and bouncy red rubber ball. For me, the funeral, any occasion to get out of the house was a holiday, like breaking suddenly from a dark tunnel into the sunlight where gardens of butterflies waited.

They had dug a grave in the red clay by the side of the road. The house was filled with people. I followed my grandparents and the dead woman's children into the room where they had laid her out, unsmiling, her nostrils stuffed with cotton. I stood in the shadows where no one saw me, filled with the smell of something I had never felt before, like a smell rising from the earth itself which no sunlight, no butterflies, no sweetness could combat. 'Miss Aggie, Miss Aggie,' I said silently to the dead old woman and suddenly I knew that if I gave her my orange to take into the unknown with her it would be safe, a secret between me and one who could return no more. I gripped the red ball tightly in my hands and it became transformed into the rough texture of an orange; I tasted it on my tongue, smelled the fragrance. As my grandmother knelt to pray I crept forward and gently placed between Miss Aggie's closed hands the love-orange, smiled because we knew each other and nothing would be able to touch either of us. But as I crept away my grandmother lifted her head from her hands and gasped when she saw the ball. She swiftly retrieved it while the others still prayed and hid it in her voluminous skirt. But when she sent me home, in anger, on the way the love-orange appeared comforting in my hand, and I went into the empty house and crept under my grandfather's bed and dreamt of worlds outside.

The next time I saw with greater clarity the vastness of this world outside. I was asked to visit some new neighbours and read to their son. He was very old, I thought, and he sat in the sunshine all day, his head covered with a calico skull cap. He couldn't see very clearly and my grandmother said he had a brain tumour and would perhaps die. Nevertheless I read to him and worried about all the knowledge that would be lost if he did not live. For every morning he would take down from a shelf a huge Atlas and together we would travel the cities of the world to which he had been. I was very happy and the names of these cities secretly rolled off my tongue all day. I wanted very much to give him my orange but held back. I was not yet sure if he were a whole person, if he would not recover and need me less and so the whole orange would be wasted. So I did not tell him about it. And then he went off with his parents to England, for an operation, my grandmother said, and he came back only as ashes held on the plane by his mother.

When I went to the church this time there was no coffin, only his mother holding this tiny box which was so like the shoe box of the doll that I was sure there was some connection which I could not grasp but I thought, if they bury this box then the broken doll cannot rise again.

But the doll rose up one more time because soon my grandmother lay dying. My mother had taken me away when she fell too ill and brought me back to my grandmother's house, even darker and more silent now, this one last time. I went into the room where she lay and she held out a weak hand to me, she couldn't speak so she followed me with her eyes and I couldn't bear it. 'Grandma,' I said quickly, searching for something to say, something that would save her, 'Grandma, you can have my whole orange,' and I placed it in the bed beside her hand. But she kept on dying and I knew then that the orange had no potency, that love could not create miracles. 'Orange,' my grandmother spoke for the last time trying to make connections that she did not see, 'orange . . . . . . ?' and my mother took me out of the room as my grandmother died. 'At least,' my mother said, 'at least you could have told her that you loved her, she waited for it'.

'But . . .' I started to say and bit my tongue, for nobody, not then or ever could understand about the orange. And in leaving my grandmother's house, the dark tunnel of my childhood, I slammed the car door hard on my fingers and as my hand closed over the breaking bones, felt nothing.

Do Angels Wear Brassieres?

Beccka down on her knees ending her goodnight prayers and Cherry telling her softly, 'And Ask God to bless Auntie Mary.' Beccka vex that anybody could interrupt her private conversation with God so, say loud loud, 'No. Not praying for nobody that tek weh mi best glassy eye marble.'

'Beccka!' Cherry almost crying in shame, 'Shhhhh! She wi hear you. Anyway she did tell you not to roll them on the floor when she have her headache.'

'A hear her already' – this is the righteous voice of Auntie Mary in the next room – 'But I am sure that God is not listening to the like of she. Blasphemous little wretch.'

She add the last part under her breath and with much lifting of her eyes to heaven she turn back to her nightly reading of the Imitations of Christ.

'Oooh Beccka, Rebecca, see what yu do,' Cherry whispering, crying in her voice.

Beccka just stick out her tongue at the world, wink at God who she know right now in the shape of a big fat anansi in a corner of the roof, kiss her mother and get into bed.

As soon as her mother gone into Auntie Mary room to try make it up and the whole night come down with whispering, Beccka whip the flash light from off the dressing table and settle down under the blanket to read. Beccka reading the Bible in secret from cover to cover not from any conviction the little wretch but because everybody round her always quoting that book and Beccka want to try and find flaw and question she can best them with.

Next morning Auntie Mary still vex. Auntie Mary out by the tank washing clothes and slapping them hard on the big rock.

59

Fat sly-eye Katie from the next yard visiting and consoling her. Everybody visiting Auntie Mary these days and consoling her for the crosses she have to bear (that is Beccka they talking about). Fat Katie have a lot of time to walk bout consoling because ever since hard time catch her son and him wife a town they come country to cotch with Katie. And from the girl walk through the door so braps! Katie claim she too sickly to do any washing or housework. So while the daughter-in-law beating suds at her yard she over by Auntie Mary washpan say she keeping her company. Right now she consoling about Beccka who (as she telling Auntie Mary) every decent-living upright Christian soul who is everybody round here except that Dorcas Waite about whom one should not dirty one's mouth to talk yes every clean living person heart go out to Auntie Mary for with all due respect to a sweet mannersable child like Cherry her daughter is the devil own pickney. Not that anybody saying a word about Cherry God know she have enough trouble on her head from she meet up that big hard back man though young little gal like that never shoulda have business with no married man. Katie take a breath long enough to ask question:

'But see here Miss Mary you no think Cherry buck up the devil own self when she carrying her? Plenty time that happen you know. Remember that woman over Allside that born the pickney with two head praise Jesus it did born dead. But see here you did know one day she was going down river to wash clothes and is the devil own self she meet. Yes'm. Standing right there in her way. She pop one big bawling before she faint weh and when everybody run come not a soul see him. Is gone he gone. But you no know where he did gone? No right inside that gal. Right inna her belly. And Miss Mary I telling you the living truth, just as the baby borning the midwife no see a shadow fly out of the mother and go right cross the room. She frighten so till she close her two eye tight and is so the devil escape.'

'Well I dont know about that. Beccka certainly dont born

with no two head or nothing wrong with her. Is just hard ears she hard ears.'

'Den no so me saying?'

'The trouble is, Cherry is too soft to manage her. As you look hard at Cherry herself she start cry. She was never a strong child and she not a strong woman, her heart just too soft.'

'All the same right is right and there is only one right way to bring up a child and that is by bus' ass pardon my french Miss Mary but hard things call for hard words. That child should be getting blows from the day she born. Then she wouldn't be so force-ripe now. Who cant hear must feel for the rod and reproof bring wisdom but a child left to himself bringeth his mother to shame. Shame, Miss Mary.'

'Is true. And you know I wouldn't mind if she did only get into mischief Miss Katie but what really hurt me is how the child know so much and show off. Little children have no right to have so many things in their brain. Guess what she ask me the other day nuh? – if me know how worms reproduce.'

'Say what, maam?'

'As Jesus is me judge. Me big woman she come and ask that. Reproduce I say. Yes Auntie Mary she say as if I stupid. When the man worm and the lady worm come together and they have baby. You know how it happen? – Is so she ask me.'

'What you saying maam? Jesus of Nazareth!'

'Yes, please. That is what the child ask me. Lightning come strike me dead if is lie I lie. In my own house. My own sister pickney. So help me I was so frighten that pickney could so impertinent that right away a headache strike me like auto-claps. But before I go lie down you see Miss Katie, I give her some licks so hot there she forget bout worm and reproduction.'

'In Jesus name!'

'Yes. Is all those books her father pack her up with. Book is all him ever good for. Rather than buy food put in the pickney mouth or help Cherry find shelter his only contribution is book. Nuh his character stamp on her. No responsibility that

man ever have. Look how him just take off for foreign without
a word even to his lawful wife and children much less Cherry
and hers. God knows where it going to end.'

'Den Miss M. They really come to live with you for all
time?'

'I dont know my dear. What are they to do? You know
Cherry cant keep a job from one day to the next. From she was
a little girl she so nervous she could never settle down long
enough to anything. And you know since Papa and Mama pass
away is me one she have to turn to. I tell you even if they eat
me out of house and home and the child drive me to Bellevue I
accept that this is the crosses that I put on this earth to bear ya
Miss Katie.'

'Amen. Anyway dont forget what I was saying to you about
the devil. The child could have a devil inside her. No pickney
suppose to come facety and force-ripe so. You better ask the
Archdeacon to check it out next time he come here.'

'Well. All the same Miss Katie she not all bad you know.
Sometime at night when she ready to sing and dance and
make up play and perform for us we laugh so till! And those
times when I watch her I say to myself, this is really a gifted
child.'

'Well my dear is your crosses. If is so you see it then is your
sister child.'

'Aie. I have one hope in God and that is the child take
scholarship exam and God know she so bright she bound to
pass. And you know what, Miss Katie, I put her name down
for the three boarding school them that furthest from here.
Make them teacher deal with her. That is what they get paid
for.'

Beccka hiding behind the tank listening to the conversation
as usual. She think about stringing a wire across the track to
trip fat Katie but she feeling too lazy today. Fat Katie will get
her comeuppance on Judgement Day for she wont able to run
quick enough to join the heavenly hosts. Beccka there thinking
of fat Katie huffing and puffing arriving at the pasture just as

the company of the faithful in their white robes are rising as one body on a shaft of light. She see Katie a-clutch at the hem of the gown of one of the faithful and miraculously, slowly, slowly, Katie start to rise. But her weight really too much and with a tearing sound that spoil the solemn moment the hem tear way from the garment and Katie fall back to earth with a big buff, shouting and wailing for them to wait on her. Beccka snickering so hard at the sight she have to scoot way quick before Auntie Mary and Katie hear her. They think the crashing about in the cocoa walk is mongoose.

Beccka in Auntie Mary room – which is forbidden – dress up in Auntie Mary bead, Auntie Mary high heel shoes, Auntie Mary shawl, and Auntie Mary big floppy hat which she only wear to wedding – all forbidden. Beccka mincing and prancing prancing and mincing in front of the three-way adjustable mirror in Auntie Mary vanity she brought all the way from Cuba with her hard earned money. Beccka seeing herself as a beautiful lady on the arms of a handsome gentleman who look just like her father. They about to enter a night club neon sign flashing for Beccka know this is the second wickedest thing a woman can do. At a corner table lit by Chinese lantern soft music playing Beccka do the wickedest thing a woman can do – she take a drink. Not rum. One day Beccka went to wedding with Auntie Mary and sneak a drink of rum and stay sick for two days. Beccka thinking of all the bright-colour drink she see advertise in the magazine Cherry get from a lady she use to work for in town a nice yellow drink in a tall frosted glass...

'Beccka, Rebecca O my God!' That is Cherry rushing into the room and wailing. 'You know she wi mad like hell if she see you with her things you know you not to touch her things.'

Cherry grab Auntie Mary things from off Beccka and fling them back into where she hope is the right place, adjust the mirror to what she hope is the right angle, and pray just pray that Auntie Mary wont find out that Beccka was messing with her things. Again. Though Auntie Mary so absolutely neat she

63

always know if a pin out of place. 'O God Beccka,' Cherry moaning.

Beccka stripped of her fancy clothes dont pay no mind to her mother fluttering about her. She take the story in her head to the room next door though here the mirror much too high for Beccka to see the sweep of her gown as she does the third wickedest thing a woman can do which is dance all night.

Auntie Mary is a nervous wreck and Cherry weeping daily in excitement. The Archdeacon is coming. Auntie Mary so excited she cant sit cant stand cant do her embroidery cant eat she forgetting things the house going to the dog she dont even notice that Beccka been using her lipstick. Again. The Archdeacon coming Wednesday to the churches in the area and afterwards – as usual – Archdeacon sure to stop outside Auntie Mary gate even for one second – as usual – to get two dozen of Auntie Mary best roses and a bottle of pimento dram save from Christmas. And maybe just this one time Archdeacon will give in to Auntie Mary pleading and step inside her humble abode for tea. Just this one time.

Auntie Mary is due this honour at least once because she is head of Mothers Union and though a lot of them jealous and back-biting her because Archdeacon never stop outside their gate even once let them say anything to her face.

For Archdeacon's certain stop outside her gate Auntie Mary scrub the house from top to bottom put up back the freshly laundered Christmas Curtains and the lace tablecloth and the newly starch doilies and the antimacassars clean all the windows in the house get the thick hibiscus hedge trim so you can skate across the top wash the dog whitewash every rock in the garden and the trunk of every tree paint the gate polish the silver and bring out the crystal cake-plate and glasses she bring from Cuba twenty-five years ago and is saving for her old age. Just in case Archdeacon can stop for tea Auntie Mary bake a fruitcake a upside-down cake a three-layer cake a chocolate cake for she dont know which he prefer also some coconut cookies for although the Archdeacon is an Englishman dont say he dont like his little Jamaican dainties. Everything will be pretty and nice for the Archdeacon just like the American lady she did work for in Cuba taught her to make them.

The only thing that now bothering Auntie Mary as she give a last look over her clean and well ordered household is Beccka, dirty Beccka right now sitting on the kitchen steps licking out the mixing bowls. The thought of Beccka in the same house with Archdeacon bring on one of Auntie Mary headache. She think of asking Cherry to take Beccka somewhere else for the afternoon when Archdeacon coming but poor Cherry work so hard and is just excited about Archdeacon coming. Auntie Mary dont have the courage to send Beccka to stay with anyone for nobody know what that child is going to come out with next and a lot of people not so broadmind as Auntie Mary. She pray that Beccka will get sick enough to have to stay in bed she – O God forgive her but is for a worthy cause – she even consider drugging the child for the afternoon. But she dont have the heart. And anyway she dont know how. So Auntie Mary take two asprin and a small glass of tonic wine and pray hard that Beccka will vanish like magic on the afternoon that Archdeacon visit.

Now Archdeacon here and Beccka and everybody in their very best clothes. Beccka thank God also on her best behaviour which can be very good so far in fact she really look like a little angel she so clean and behaving.

In fact Archdeacon is quite taken with Beccka and more and more please that this is the afternoon he decide to consent to come inside Auntie Mary parlour for one little cup of tea. Beccka behaving so well and talking so nice to the Archdeacon Auntie Mary feel her heart swell with pride and joy over everything. Beccka behaving so beautiful in fact that Auntie Mary and Cherry dont even think twice about leaving her to talk to Archdeacon in the parlour while they out in the kitchen preparing tea.

By now Beccka and the Archdeacon exchanging Bible knowledge. Beccka asking him question and he trying his best to answer but they never really tell him any of these things in theological college. First he go ask Beccka if she is a good little girl. Beccka say yes she read her Bible every day. Do you now say the Archdeacon, splendid. Beccka smile and look shy.

'Tell me my little girl, is there anything in the Bible you would like to ask me about?'

'Yes sir. Who in the Bible wrote big?'

'Who in the Bible wrote big. My dear child!'

This wasnt the kind of question Archdeacon expecting but him always telling himself how he have rapport with children so he decide to confess his ignorance.

'Tell me, who?'

'Paul!' Beccka shout.

'Paul?'

'Galations six eleven "See with how large letters I write onto you with mine own hands".'

'Ho Ho Ho Ho' Archdeacon laugh. – 'Well done. Try me with another one.'

Beccka decide to ease him up this time.

'What animal saw an angel?'

'What animal saw an angel? My word. What animal ... of course. Balaam's Ass.'

'Yes you got it.'

Beccka jumping up and down she so excited. She decide to ask the Archdeacon a trick questions her father did teach her.

'What did Adam and Eve do when they were driven out of the garden?'

'Hm,' the Archdeacon sputtered but could not think of a suitable answer.

'Raise Cain ha ha ha ha ha.'

'They raised Cain Ho Ho Ho Ho Ho.'

The Archdeacon promise himself to remember that one to tell the Deacon. All the same he not feeling strictly comfortable. It really dont seem dignified for an Archdeacon to be having this type of conversation with an eleven-year-old girl. But Beccka already in high gear with the next question and Archdeacon tense himself.

'Who is the shortest man in the Bible?'

Archdeacon groan.

'Peter. Because him sleep on his watch. Ha Ha Ha'.

'Ho Ho Ho Ho Ho Ho.'

'What is the smallest insect in the Bible?'

'The widow's mite,' Archdeacon shout.

'The wicked flee,' Beccka cry.

'Ho Ho Ho Ho Ho Ho.'

Archdeacon laughing so hard now he starting to cough. He cough and cough till the coughing bring him to his senses. He there looking down the passage where Auntie Mary gone and wish she would hurry come back. He sputter a few time into his handkerchief, wipe his eye, sit up straight and assume his most religious expression. Even Beccka impress.

'Now Rebecca. Hm. You are a very clever very entertaining little girl. Very. But what I had in mind were questions that are a bit more serious. Your aunt tells me you are being prepared for confirmation. Surely you must have some questions about doctrine hm, religion, that puzzle you. No serious questions?'

Beccka look at Archdeacon long and hard. 'Yes,' she say at long last in a small voice. Right away Archdeacon sit up straighter.

'What is it my little one?'

Beccka screwing up her face in concentration.

'Sir, what I want to know is this for I cant find it in the Bible. Please sir, do angels wear brassieres?'

Auntie Mary just that minute coming through the doorway with a full tea tray with Cherry carrying another big tray right behind her. Enough food and drink for ten Archdeacon. Auntie Mary stop braps in the dooway with fright when she hear Beccka question. She stop so sudden that Cherry bounce into her and spill a whole pitcher of cold drink all down Auntie

Mary back. As the coldness hit her Auntie Mary jump and half her tray throw way on the floor milk and sugar and sandwiches a rain down on Archdeacon. Archdeacon jump up with his handkerchief and start mop himself and Auntie Mary at the same time he trying to take the tray from her. Auntie Mary at the same time trying to mop up the Archdeacon with a napkin in her mortification not even noticing how Archdeacon relieve that so much confusion come at this time. Poor soft-hearted Cherry only see that her sister whole life ruin now she dont yet know the cause run and sit on the kitchen stool and throw kitchen cloth over her head and sit there bawling and bawling in sympathy.

Beccka win the scholarship to high school. She pass so high she getting to go to the school of Auntie Mary choice which is the one that is furthest away. Beccka vex because she dont want go no boarding school with no heap of girl. Beccka dont want to go to no school at all.

Everyone so please with Beccka. Auntie Mary even more please when she get letter from the headmistress setting out Rules and Regulation. She only sorry that the list not longer for she could think of many things she could add. She get another letter setting out uniform and right away Auntie Mary start sewing. Cherry take the bus to town one day with money coming from God know where for the poor child dont have no father to speak of and she buy shoes and socks and underwear and hair ribbon and towels and toothbrush and a suitcase for Beccka. Beccka normally please like puss with every new thing vain like peacock in ribbons and clothes. Now she hardly look at them. Beccka thinking. She dont want to go to no school. But how to get out of it. When Beccka think done she decide to run away and find her father who like a miracle have job now in a circus. And as Beccka find him so she get job in the circus as a tight-rope walker and in spangles and tights lipstick and powder (her own) Beccka perform every night before a cheering crowd in a blaze of light. Beccka and the circus go right round the world. Every now and then, dress up in furs and hats like Auntie Mary wedding hat Beccka come home to visit Cherry and Auntie Mary. She arrive in a chauffeur-driven limousine pile high with luggage. Beccka shower them with presents. The whole village. For fat Katie Beccka bring a years supply of diet pill and a exercise machine just like the one she see advertise in the magazine the lady did give to Cherry.

Now Beccka ready to run away. In the books, the picture always show children running away with their things tied in a bundle on a stick. The stick easy. Beccka take one of the walking stick that did belong to Auntie Mary's dear departed. Out of spite she take Auntie Mary silk scarf to wrap her things in for Auntie Mary is to blame for her going to school at all. She pack in the bundle Auntie Mary lipstick Auntie Mary face powder and a pair of Auntie Mary stockings for she need these for her first appearance as a tight rope walker. She take a slice of cake, her shiny eye marble and a yellow nicol which is her best taa in case she get a chance to play in the marble championship of the world. She also take the Bible. She want to find some real hard question for the Archdeacon next time he come to Auntie Mary house for tea.

When Auntie Mary and Cherry busy sewing her school clothes Beccka take off with her bundle and cut across the road into the field. Mr. O'Connor is her best friend and she know he wont mind if she walk across his pasture. Mr. O'Connor is her best friend because he is the only person Beccka can hold a real conversation with. Beccka start to walk toward the mountain that hazy in the distance. She plan to climb the mountain and when she is high enough she will look for a sign that will lead her to her father. Beccka walk and walk through the pasture divided by stone wall and wooden gates which she climb: Sometime a few trees tell her where a pond is. But it is very lonely. All Beccka see is john crow and cow and cattle egret blackbird and parrotlets that scream at her from the trees. But Beccka dont notice them. Her mind busy on how Auntie Mary and Cherry going to be sad now she gone and she composing letter she will write to tell them she safe and she forgive them everything. But the sun getting too high in the sky and Beccka thirsty. She eat the cake but she dont have water. Far in the distance she see a bamboo clump and hope is round a spring with water. But when she get to the bamboo all it offer is shade. In fact the dry bamboo leaves on the ground so soft and inviting that Beccka decide to sit and rest for a while. Is sleep Beccka sleep. When she wake she see a stand above her four horse leg and when she raise up and look, stirrups, boots, and sitting atop the horse her best friend, Mr. O'Connor.

'Well Beccka, taking a long walk?'

'Yes sir.'

'Far from home eh?'

'Yes sir.'

'Running away?'

'Yes sir.'

'Hm. What are you taking with you?'

Beccka tell him what she have in the bundle. Mr. O'Connor shock.

'What, no money?'

'Oooh!'

Beccka shame like anything for she never remember anything about money.

'Well you need money for running away you know. How else you going to pay for trains and planes and taxis and buy ice cream and pindar cake?'

Beccka didn't think about any of these things before she run away. But now she see that is sense Mr. O'Connor talking but she dont know what to do. So the two of them just stand up there for a while. They thinking hard.

'You know Beccka if I was you I wouldnt bother with the running away today. Maybe they dont find out you gone yet. So I would go back home and wait until I save enough money to finance my journey.'

Beccka love how that sound. To finance my journey. She think about that a long time. Mr. O'Connor say, 'Tell you what. Why don't you let me give you a ride back and you can pretend this was just a practice and you can start saving your money to run away properly next time.'

Beccka look at Mr. O'Connor. He looking off into the distance and she follow where he gazing and when she see the mountain she decide to leave it for another day. All the way back riding with Mr. O'Connor Beccka thinking and thinking and her smile getting bigger and bigger. Beccka cant wait to get home to dream up all the tricky question she could put to a whole school full of girl. Not to mention the teachers. Beccka laughing for half the way home. Suddenly she say –

'Mr. Connor, you know the Bible?'

'Well Beccka I read my Bible every day so I should think so.'

'Promise you will answer a question.'

'Promise.'

'Mr. Connor, do angels wear brassieres?'

'Well Beccka, as far as I know only the lady angels need to.'

Beccka laugh cant done. Wasnt that the answer she was waiting for?

The Boy Who Loved Ice Cream

They walked down the path in single file, first the father carrying the baby Beatrice on his shoulder, then the mother, then Elsa. He brought up the rear. Wearing unaccustomed sandals, Benjy found it hard to keep his footing on the slippery path. Once or twice he almost fell and throwing out his hands to break his fall, had touched the ground. Unconsciously he wiped his hands on his seat, so that his new Sunday-go-to-church pants that his mother had made from cutting down one of his father's old jackets was already dirty with bits of mud and green bush clinging to him. But there was nobody behind him to see.

They were already late for the Harvest Festival Sale, or so his father claimed. Papa also said that it was his fault. But then his father blamed him for a lot of things, even when he was not to be blamed. The boy wasn't sure why his father was sometimes so irritable towards him, and lived in a constant state of suspense over what his father's response to him was likely to be. Now, he had been the first ready. First . his sister had taken him around to the side of the house for his bath. She held him and firmly scrubbed him down with a 'strainer' covered in soap. Then she had stuck the long-handled dipper into the drum of rain water and poured it over him from head to foot. He made noises as the cold water hit him and would have run, but Elsa always had a firm grip on one of his limbs.

'Stan still yu jumbo-head bwoy or a konk yu till yu fenny,' she hissed at him. Although he knew that her threats were infrequently accompanied by action beyond a slap or two, still he tried to get away from her grip for he hated this weekly ritual of bathing. But Elsa by now had learned to control him and she carried the bath through without mishap for she had whispered, 'Awright. Doan have yu bath and see what happen. See if yu get no ice cream'.

Ice Cream! The very words conveyed to him the sound of everything in his life that he had always wanted, always longed for, but could not give a name to. He had never tasted ice cream.

It was Elsa who had told him about it. Two years ago at the Harvest Festival Sale, Mr. Doran had brought an ice cream bucket and had spent the evening the most popular man at the sale, his very customers fighting to get an opportunity to turn the bucket. According to Elsa's description, this marvellous bucket somehow produced something that, she said, was not a drink and was not food. It was hot and it was cold. Both at the same time. You didn't chew it, but if you held it on your tongue long enough it vanished, leaving an after-trace that lingered and lingered like a beautiful dream. Elsa the excitable, the imaginative, the self-assured, told him, think of your best dream, when he didn't understand. Think of it in colours, she said, pink and mauve and green. And imagine it with edges. Then imagine licking it slowly round and round the edges. That's how ice cream was.

But this description only bewildered him more. He sighed, and tried hard to imagine it. But he couldn't because he didn't have a best dream or even a good dream, only nightmares, and his mother would hold him and his father would say, 'what is wrong with this pickney eh? a mampala man yu a raise'. Then the baby had come and he didn't have his mother's lap any more. Now imagining ice cream, he thought of sitting cuddled in his mother's arms again and saw this mysterious new creation as something as warm and beautiful. From Elsa's description, ice cream was the most marvellous thing he had ever heard of. And the strangest. For apart from anything else, he didn't know what ice was. His thoughts kept returning to the notion of ice cream throughout the year, and soon it became the one bright constant in a world full of changeable adults.

Then last year when he would have discovered for himself exactly what this ice cream was like, he had come down with measles. Elsa of course went to the sale for she had already had it, but he had to stay feverish and miserable with only toothless old Tata Maud to keep him company. And Elsa had come back and given him a description of ice cream that was even more marvellous than the first. This time Mr. Doran had brought two buckets, and she alone had had two cones. Not even the drops, the wangla, and the slice of light cake they brought him could compensate for missing the ice cream.

This year he was well and nothing would keep him away.

Now with the thought of ice cream the cold water his sister kept splashing on him felt refreshing and he and she turned the bath into a game, both shrieking so loudly that their mother had to put her head out the window and promise to switch them both if they didn't stop.

His mother rubbed him down with an old cloth and put on his new clothes of which he was extremely proud, not noticing that the black serge was stitched very badly with white thread which was all his mother had, and the three buttons she sewed down the front were all of different sizes and colours. His shirt too, with the body of one colour, the sleeves of a print which was once part of mama's dress and the collar of yet another print, was just, Mama said, like Joseph's coat of many colours.

Then Mama had dressed the baby and she herself had got ready. By this time Papa had come up from the spring where he had had his bath and put on his Sunday suit and hat. Benjy, dressed and bored, had wandered off down to the cotton tree root to have another look at the marvellous colours and shapes of the junjo which had sprung up after the rains just a few days ago. He was so busy that it took him a long time to hear them calling. They were standing all ready to go to the Harvest Festival Sale and Papa was cross for he said that Benjy was making them late.

Papa dressed in his Sunday suit and hat was a sight to see, for he only dressed up for special occasions – funerals, weddings and the Harvest Festival Sale. Papa never went to church though Mama did every Sunday. Papa complained every Sunday that there was no hot food and dinner was always late for Mama never got back from church till late afternoon. Plus Papa never liked Mama to be away from him for any length of time.

Foolishness, foolishness, Papa said of the church going.

Mama didn't say anything but she prayed for Papa every Sunday. She wasn't that religious, but she loved every opportunity to go out. She loved to dress up and she loved to talk to people and hear all the news that was happening out there in the wide world, though she didn't believe half of it. Although Mama hadn't even been to Kingston in her life, if someone came along and said, 'Let us go to the moon,' quick as anything Mama would pick herself up and go. Or if Papa said to her 'Let us give up all this hard life and move to town where we will have electric light and water out of a pipe and food out of a tin,' Mama would not hesitate. Papa of course would never dream of saying anything of the sort. He was firmly wedded to the soil. She was always for Progress, though, as she sadly complained to the children, none of that ever came their way.

Now the Harvest Festival Sale was virtually the only time that Papa went into Springville these days. He hated to go into Springville even though it was where he was born for increasingly over the last four or five years, he had developed the feeling that Springville people knew something he didn't know but should, and they were laughing at him behind his back. It was something to do with his woman. It was one of those entirely intuitive feelings that suddenly occurred full-blown, then immediately took firm root in the mind. Even before the child was born he had had the instinctive feeling that it was not his. Then as the boy had grown, he had searched his face, his features, to discern himself there, and had failed utterly to find anything conclusive. He could never be sure. The old women used to say you could tell paternity sure thing by comparing the child's foot with that of the supposed father: 'if the foot not the spitting image of the man then is jacket'. He had spent countless surreptitious hours studying the turn of his son's foot but had come away with nothing. For one thing, the child was so thin and rickety that his limbs bore no resemblance to the man's heavily muscled body.

Now he had never known of the woman being unfaithful to him. But the minute she had come back from spending three weeks in Springville that time her mother was dying, from then on he had had the feeling that something had happened. Maybe it was only because she seemed to him so beautiful, so womanly that he had the first twinges of jealousy. Now every Sunday as she dressed in her neat white dress and shoes and the chaste hat which to him sat so provocatively on her head, his heart quickened as he saw her anew, not as the young girl he had taken from her mother's house so many years before, not as the gentle and good-natured mother of his children, but as a woman whom he suddenly perceived as a being attractive to other men.

But now everyone was in a good mood again as they set off down the road to the Harvest Festival Sale. First they walked a mile and a half down their mountain path where they saw no one, until they met up with the main path to the village. Always in the distance ahead of them now they could see people similarly dressed going to the sale. Others would call out to them from their houses as they passed by:

'Howdy Mis Dinah,' said Papa.

'Mis Dinah,' Mama said.

'Mis Dinah,' the children murmured.

'Howdy Mister Seeter. Miss Mae. Children. Yu gone on early.'

'Ai. Yu coming?'

'No mus'. Jus a wait for Icy finish iron mi frock Mis Mac. A ketch yu up soon.'

'Awright Mis D.'

Then they would walk another quarter mile or so till they got to another house perched on the hillside.

'Owdy Mister Seeter. Miss Mae. Little ones. A coming right behin.'

And another family group would come out of the house and join them. Soon, a long line of people was walking in single file down the path. The family groups got mixed. The adults would walk behind other adults so that they could talk. The children bringing up the rear instinctively ranked themselves, putting the smallest ones in front. Occasionally one of the adults would look back and frown because the tail of the line had fallen too far behind.

'Stop! Jacky! Ceddie! Mavis! Merteen! What yu all doing back there a lagga lagga so? Jus' hurry up ya pickney.'

Then all the offspring chastised, the adults would soon become lost in a discussion of the tough-headedness of children.

The children paid hardly any attention and even forgot to fight or get into any mischief, for they were far too excited about the coming afternoon.

Soon, the path broadened out and joined the lane which led to the Commons where the sale was being held. Benjy loved to come out from the cool and shadows of the path, through an archway of wild brazilwood with branches that drooped so much the adults had to lift them up in order to get through. From the semi-darkness they came suddenly into the broad lane covered in marl and dazzling white which to him was the broadest street in the whole world. Today the lane was full of people as far as the eye could see, all the men in their dark suits and hats and the women, abandoning their chaste Sunday white, wearing their brightest dresses. Now a new set of greetings had to take place between the mountain people who came from a place called One Eye and were regarded as 'dark' and mysterious by the people who lived in the one-time prosperous market town of Springville. Springville itself wasn't much – a crossroads with a few wooden 'upstairs' houses with fretwork balconies, built at the turn of the century with quick money made in Panama or Cuba. Now even though these houses were so old they leaned in the wind together, and had never seen a coat of paint, to the mountain people they looked as huge and magical as anything they hoped to see. Two of these upstairs houses had shops and bars beneath, with their proud owners residing above, and on one corner there was a large one-storey concrete building with huge wooden shutters which housed the Chinese grocery and the Chinese. A tiny painted house served as the post office and the equally tiny house beside it housed Brother Brammie the tailor. The most imposing buildings in the village were the school and the Anglican Church which were both on the main lane. The Baptists and the Seventh Day Adventists had their churches on the side road.

At Harvest Festival time, all the people in the village forgot their differences and came together to support each other's Harvest Festival Sales. But none could compare in magnificence to the Anglicans'. The sale took place on the Monday after the Harvest Service in the church. On Monday morning at dawn, the church members travelled from far with the bamboo poles and coconut boughs to erect on the Commons the booths for the sale. Because the sale was a secular event and liable to attract all kinds of sinners, it was not held in the church yard but on the Commons which belonged to the church but was separated by a barbed wire fence. Since the most prosperous people in the area were Anglicans, this was the largest and most popular of the sales. After a while it became less of a traditional Harvest Festival Sale and more of a regular fair, for people began to come from the city with goods to sell, and took over a little corner of the Commons for themselves. The church people frowned on this at first, then gave up on keeping these people out even when they began to bring games such as 'Crown and Anchor', for they helped to attract larger and larger crowds which also spent money in the church members' booths. The church members also enjoyed themselves buying the wares of the town vendors, parson drawing the line only at the sale and consumption of liquor on the premises. A few zealots of the village strongly objected to this sale, forbidding their daughters to go to this den of wickedness and vice, but nobody paid these people the slightest attention. The Mothers' Union ladies who had decorated the church for the Harvest Service the day before now tied up sprays of bougainvillea and asparagus fern over the entrance into each booth and radiated good cheer to everyone in their self-appointed role as hostesses.

The sale actually started at noon, but the only people who got there early were those who were involved in the arrangements. Most people turned up only after the men had put in at least a half-day in the fields and then gone home to bathe and dress and eat. They would stay at the sale until night had fallen, using bottle torches to light their way home.

When they got to the Commons, Benjy was the only person who was worried, for he wasn't sure that they wouldn't get there too late for the ice cream. Maybe Mr. Doran would make the ice cream as soon as the sale started and then it would all be finished by the time they got there. Then another thought came: suppose this year Mr. Doran was sick, or simply couldn't be bothered with ice cream any more. He would have to wait a whole year again to taste it. Perhaps never.

'Suppose, jus' suppose,' he had said to his sister many times during the past week, 'suppose him doan mek enough.'

'Cho! As soon as him finish wan bucket him mek anadda. Ice cream nevva done,' Elsa told him impatiently, wishing that she had never brought up the subject.

But this did not console him. Suppose his father refused to buy him ice cream? It was unthinkable! And yet his father's behaviour towards him was irrational: Benjy never knew just what to expect.

As soon as they turned into the Commons they could hear the sound of Mass Vass' accordion rising shrilly above the noise of the crowd, as much a part of the Harvest Festival sale

79

as was Brother Shearer's fife and drum band that played at all fairs, weddings and other notable events for miles around.

There were so many people already in the Commons that Benjy was afraid to enter: the crowd was a living, moving thing that would swallow him up as soon as he crossed through the gate. And yet he was excited too, and his excitement won out over his fear so that he boldly stepped up to the gate where the ticket taker waited and Papa paid the entrance fee for them all.

'Now you children dont bother get lost,' Mama warned them but not too sternly, knowing that sooner or later they would all become separated in this joyous crowd.

Benjy was in an agony just to see the ice cream. But Elsa would have none of it.

'Wait nuh,' she said, grabbing his hand and steering him firmly in the direction of the fancy goods stall where Mama had headed. There were cake stalls and pickles and preserves stalls, fancy goods stalls, glass cases full of baked goods and all the finest in fruits, vegetables, yams and all the other products of the soil that the people had brought to the church as their offerings to the Harvest Service. Off to one side was a small wooden merry-go-round and all over the field were children playing and shrieking.

'Elsa, ice cream,' Benjy kept saying, and finally to reduce this annoyance Elsa took him over to a corner of the field where a crowd had gathered. There, she said. But the crowd was so thick that he could see nothing, and he felt a pain in his heart that so many other, bigger people also wanted ice cream. How ever would he get any?

'Nuh mine, Benjy,' Elsa consoled him. 'Papa wi gi wi ice cream. When de time come.'

'Suppose him forget, Elsa.'

'Not gwine forget.'

'Yu remin' him.'

'Yes.'

'Promise?'

'But wa do yu ee bwoy,' Elsa cried. She angrily flung his hand away and took off into the crowd.

He did not mind being alone, for this rich crowd so flowed that sooner or later the same people passed each other.

Benjy wished he had some money. Then he would go and wiggle his way into the very centre of the crowd that surrounded the ice cream bucket. And he would be standing there just as Mr. Doran took out the ice cream. But he didn't know anything about money and had no idea what something as wonderful as ice cream would cost.

So he flowed with the crowd, stopping here and there but not really looking at anything and soon he came across his mother with Beatrice. Mama firmly took hold of his hand.

'Come. Sister Nelson bring a piece of pone fe yu.'

She took him to Sister Nelson who gave him the pone which he stuffed into his mouth.

'Say tank yu chile. Yu doan have manners?' his mother asked.

He murmured thank you through the pone. Sister Nelson smiled at him. 'Growing a good boy,' she said and patted his head.

'But baad!' Mama said, laughing.

Mama was always saying that and it frightened him a little, for he never knew for sure just how he was 'baad'.

'Mama,' he said, 'ice cream.'

'Chile! Yu mout full an yu talking bout ice cream aready!'

Tears started to trickle down his cheeks.

'Now see here. A bawl yu wan' bawl? Doan mek a give yu something fe bawl bout, yu hear bwoy. Hm. Anyway a doan know if there is money for foolishness like cream. Have to see yu father about dat.'

His heart sank, for the day before he had heard his father complain that there was not enough money to buy all the things they needed at the Harvest Festival Sale and did she think money grew on trees. But everyone knew that Papa saved all year for that day, for the town vendors came and spread out their wares under the big cotton tree – cloth, pots and pans, fancy lamps, wicks and shades, readymade clothes, shoes, shoelaces, matches, knives, cheap perfume, plastic oil-cloths for the table, glasses with birds and flowers, water jugs, needles, enamelware, and plaster wall hangings with robins and favourite Bible texts. Even Miss Sybil who had the dry goods store would turn up and buy from them, and months later the goods would turn up in her dark and dusty shop at twice the price as the vendors'.

Mama had announced months in advance that she wanted an oilskin cloth, a new lampshade and shoes for the children. She hadn't mentioned anything for herself, but on these occasions Mama usually came home with a pair of new shoes, or a scarf, or a hat – anything that would put her in touch with what seemed another, glamorous life.

Papa, like his son, was distracted, torn between two desires. One was to enjoy the sale and to see if he could pick up anything for the farm or just talk to the farmers whom nowadays he never saw at any other time. Then the Extension Officer was there and he wanted to catch him to ask about some new thing he had heard that the government was lending money to plant crops though he didn't believe a word of it. Then he wanted to go and buy a good white shirt from the town vendors. Mama had insisted that he should. And he wanted to see the new games they had brought. In many ways one part of his mind was like a child's, for he wanted to see and do everything. But another part of his mind was spoiling the day for him: he didn't want to let Mama out of his sight. More and more the conviction had been growing on him that if there had been another man in her life, it wasn't anyone from around here. So it had to be a townman. And where else did one get the opportunity to meet strangers but at the sale. Walking down the mountain path he had started out enjoying the feeling of going on an outing, the only one he permitted himself for the year. But as they got nearer and nearer to

Springville and were joined by other people, he became more and more uneasy. The way his woman easily greeted and chatted with people at first used to fill him with pride and admiration that she could so naturally be at ease where he was dull and awkward and clumsy. But by the time they entered the lane this pride had turned to irritation, for now he had begun to exaggerate in his mind precisely those qualities for which he had previously praised her: now she laughed too loudly, chattered too much, she was not modest enough, she attracted attention to herself – and to him, for having a woman so common and so visible. By the time they got to the Commons it was clear to her that he was in one of his 'moods' though she did not know why and she hoped that the crowd would bring back his good humour again, for she was accustomed to his ups and downs. But she didn't dwell on the man's moods, for nothing would make her not enjoy herself at the sale.

Now the man surreptitiously tried to keep her under his eye but it was virtually impossible because of the crowd. He saw her sometimes only as a flash in the distance and he strained to see what she was up to, but he caught her only in the most innocent of poses – with church sisters and married couples and little children. She eagerly tried on hats and shoes. She looked at pictures. She examined tablecloths. She ate grater cake and snowballs. Looking at her from afar, her gestures seemed to him so pure, so innocent that he told himself that he was surely mad to think badly of her. Then he looked at the town folk gathered around the games, hawking yards of cloth, and stockings and ties and cheap jewellery. He looked at them and their slim hard bodies and their stylish clothes and their arrogant manners and their tough faces which hid a knowledge of the world he could never have. And he felt anxious and angry again. Now he turned all his attention to these townmen to see if he could single out one of them: the one. So engaged did he become on this lonely and futile pursuit that he hardly heard at all what anybody said to him. Even the children begging for ice cream he roughly brushed aside. He was immediately full of remorse, for he had planned to treat them to ice cream, but by the time he came to his senses and called after them, they had disappeared into the crowd. He vowed that once he met up with them again he would make up for his gruffness. He would treat them not only to ice cream but to sliced cake, to soft drinks, to paradise plums and jujubs. But the moment of softness, of sentiment, quickly passed for his attention became focussed on one man in black pants and a purple shirt and wearing a grey felt hat. The man was tall, brown-skinned and good looking with dark, curly hair. He couldn't tell why this man caught his attention except that he was by far the best looking of the townmen, seemed in fact a cut above them, even though like some of the others his arms were covered from wrist to elbow in lengths of cheap chains, and his fingers in the tacky rings that he was selling. He watched the man steadily while he flirted and chatted with the girls and finally faded out of sight – but not in the direction his woman was last seen.

Now Benjy was crying and even Elsa felt let down. Papa had refused to buy them ice cream! Although she cajoled and threatened, she couldn't get Benjy to stop crying. He was crying as much for the ice cream as for being lost from even his mother so happy and animated among all the people she knew, amid crowds and noise and confusion. Now she had little time for them and impatiently waved them on to 'enjoy themselves'. Elsa did just that for she found everything entertaining and school friends to chatter with. But not Benjy. She could not understand how a little boy could be so lacking in joy for such long periods of time, and how his mind could become focussed on just one thing. If Benjy could not have ice cream, he wanted nothing.

Night was coming on and they were lighting the lamps. They hung up the storm lantern at the gate but all the coconut

booths were lit with kitchen bitches. Only the cake stall run by
Parson's wife and the most prosperous ladies of the church had
a tilly lamp, though there wasn't much cake left to sell.

Benjy still stumbled along blindly, dragged by Elsa who was
determined to get a last fill of everything. Benjy was no longer
crying but his eyes were swollen and he was tired and his feet
were dragging. He knew that soon they would have to go
home. The lighting of the lamps was the signal for gathering
up families together, and though they might linger for a while
after that talking, making last minute purchases and plans,
children were at this point not allowed to wander or stray from
the group for the word of adults had once again become law,
and when all the adults decided to move, woe unto the child
who could not be found.

So everyone was rounding up everyone else, and in this
confusion, Benjy started to howl again for he and Elsa were
passing by Mr. Doran and his bucket, only the crowd was so
thick around it you couldn't see anything.

But just then they ran into Papa again and, miraculously, he
was the one that suggested ice cream. Although Benjy's spirits
immediately lifted, he still felt anxious that Papa would never
be able to get through that crowd in time. Papa left him and
Elsa on the fringes, and he impatiently watched as Papa, a big
man, bore his way through. What is taking Papa so long? I bet
Mr. Doran has come to the end of the bucket. There is no more
ice cream. Here comes Mr. Manuel and Mars Edgy asking if
they aren't ready. And indeed, everyone from the mountain
was more or less assembled and they and Papa now seemed
the only people missing from the group. They told Mars Edgy
that Papa had gone to get them ice cream, and Mars Edgy was
vexed because, he said, Papa should have done that long
before. Now Mars Edgy made his way through the crowd
around the ice cream vendor and Benjy's hopes fell again. He
felt sure that Mars Edgy would pull Papa away before he got
the ice cream. Torn between hope and despair, Benjy looked
up at the sky which was pink and mauve from the setting sun.

Just like ice cream! But here comes Papa and Mars Edgy now and Papa is carrying in his hands three cones and Papa is coming and Benjy is so excited that he starts to run towards him and he stumbles and falls and Elsa is laughing as she picks him up and he is laughing and Mars Edgy is moving off quickly to where the mountain people are standing and Papa bends down and hands him a cone and Papa has a cone and Elsa has a cone and Benjy has a cone and the three of them stand there as if frozen in time and he is totally joyous for he is about to have his first taste of ice cream but even though this is so long-awaited so precious he first has to hold the cone at arm's length to examine it and witness the ice cream perched just so on top and he is afraid to put it into his mouth for Elsa said it was colder than spring water early in the morning and suppose just suppose it burns his tongue suppose he doesn't like it and Elsa who is well into eating hers and Papa who is eating his are laughing at him ... then he doesn't know what is happening for suddenly Papa sees something his face quickly changes and he flings away his cone and makes a grab for Benjy and starts walking almost running in the direction where Mama is standing she is apart from all the people talking to a strange man in a purple shirt and Papa is moving so fast Benjy's feet are almost off the ground and Benjy is crying Papa Papa and everything is happening so quickly he doesn't know the point at which he loses the ice cream and half the cone and all that is left in his hand is the little tip of the cone which he clutches tightly and he cannot understand why Papa has let go of his hand and is shouting and why Mama isn't laughing with the man anymore and why everyone is rushing about and why he has only this little tip of cone in his hand and there is no ice cream and he cannot understand why the sky which a minute ago was pink and mauve just like the ice cream is now swimming in his vision like one swollen blanket of rain.

The stories of
Lorna Goodison

The Dolly Funeral

I can't remember how Bev and I became friends, but I remember at first feeling displaced by her as leader of our neighbourhood group of children at large, in the summer holidays. She came from a family that was even bigger than mine and up until that time I had been the child to hold that particular distinction. I had six brothers which meant people thought twice about interfering with me. Bev had eight brothers. My parents had nine children. There were twelve children in the Lyons' household, and when her family moved into the neighbourhood, she just naturally assumed the leadership role which I had held till then. I loved visiting the Lyons' house. They lived in 'their own place', which made them rich in the eyes of everyone in the neighbourhood. Their place was a many-roomed yard which was peopled by the many Lyons' married sons and daughters and a few aunts and cousins.

The first time I visited their house, I remember wishing that I lived there. Unlike my house, where somebody was always correcting you for 'sitting down bad' or 'common behaviour', the Lyons were a marvellously free and uninhibited people.

They yelled at each other, screamed with laughter and used language that would send my mother for the brown soap to scour out somebody's mouth.

The first time I witnessed Mrs. Lyons trying to discipline Vavan, 'the baby' of the family, I was truly astonished. Vavan did some really dreadful thing, Mrs. Lyons screamed at him to 'beyave,' he replied 'Gweyframme'. She swung a punch at him, he stuck out his tongue at her, dropped to his belly, wriggled under the bed and from his dark hideout proceeds to tell her some things no child should tell a mother and remain alive. She yelled that she was going to tear his backside and seizing a broom proceeded to stab wildly at his hidden form. She must have seen me staring at her because she paused and advised me to go outside and play in the yard, then they resumed the duel, he with the foul mouth and she with the broomstick.

All sorts of wonderful things happened at the Lyons' house. Periodic fights would break out between the brothers: big, strong Spanish-looking men, who would fight each other fiercely until their mother appeared and sometimes doused them with a goblet of cold water.

My friend Bev had all sorts of lovely toys and games to play with, but mostly she had a wonderful talent for organizing great events. These could range from the really low-level act of getting a group of children together to go and tease Rowena – the retarded child who lived several streets away (I can truly say I could never bring myself to join in this activity), to informing on Mr. Frenchie to his wife, Miss Dolly, about which bar he had spent all his money in (she always told her to mind her own business and stay out of big people's business), to organizing dolls' tea parties, weddings and pregnancies, to the Dolly Funeral.

One day, towards the end of the summer holidays when it seemed we had run out of new games to play and that Bev's reputation for inspiring leadership of our group was beginning to pall, Bev came up with the idea of the Dolly Funeral. She proceeded to kill one of her less attractive dolls, by wringing its rubber neck, and placing it in a shoe box on her bed... 'She dead,' said Bev in a low voice, 'we going to have to bury her.' For two days the doll lay in the 'dead house' as Bev referred to the shoe box, her life all bubbled out in clouds of pink and white foam, while we prepared for the Funeral.

We searched my mother's sewing scraps for some white satin and lace material and we sewed her a lovely shroud. Bev's brother Harry proceeded to nail up a crude coffin using what looked like boards ripped from the side of the pit latrine; all arrangements for the funeral were organized by Bev.

First there would be a procession from the front gate through the middle gate (her yard had two separate sections) and down to the graveside which was situated under a huge ackee tree. I was not so thrilled to hear about the choice of this site as large rats were known to live in the ackee tree and I was more afraid of them than most other things, but I had to go along with Bev's plans.

We all went to inspect the grave site which had been dug by Harry, Bev's brother, with one of Mrs. Lyons' cooking spoons. There were to be some light refreshments as it was necessary to attract as many children as possible to this event. The refreshments consisted of pieces of bulla cake and lime-less limeade known as belly-wash.

The funeral arrangements fully occupied us for two days. Bev was going to be the parson; when the boys remarked that nobody had ever seen a woman parson, she just looked at them and said, 'Is whose dolly funeral?' and they retreated. I was going to read from the Bible because I could read better than any of the other children, or so they said anyway.

My mother was not consistent when it came to allowing me to play at other people's houses. Some days for no reason, she would say, 'Don't leave the house today, sometimes you should let people long to see you.' The day of the funeral was one of those days. I got dressed to walk over to Bev's house and as I approached my mother to ask her permission/inform her where I was going, she said 'Don't leave the house, etc...' I pleaded with her, I enquired of her if she did not remember me telling her all about the arrangements for the funeral, how important it was that I go because I was going to read from the Bible and could she 'just please do, I beg you, mama, make me go'. My mother started the sewing machine by slapping the rim of the handle with her palm and proceeded to pump the broad flat pedal at a fierce rate. That action, read by any fool, clearly meant, 'Don't say anymore.'

So I subsided in a corner of the verandah and wept. As with each time I felt I had been dealt an injustice by my parents, I imagined that I was not their child. That I had been the victim of a careless hospital blunder and that my real parents were out there somewhere in Kingston. Nice people, who would never deprive me of the right to attend a Dolly Funeral.

As the time of the funeral approached, Bev came over to enquire why I was not present at the site, and saw me sobbing in a corner of the verandah. I told her what my mother had said, she said, hissing her teeth, 'Chuh just teef out,' and I for the first time in my life did just that, I sneaked out of the yard without my mother's permission. But I had to do it in stages. When Bev had left, I got up from my corner (after a suitable period of time) and made my move, first, to the cistern where I drank some water I did not want, then from the cistern when Miss Minnie our helper's back was turned, to the back gate where I stood for some time looking forlornly over the zinc fences and across the gully.

After stage three came the quick, bold dash to freedom. As I took to my heels and headed for Bev's house looking in no other direction but straight ahead, was it paranoia or did I really hear Miss Minnie calling, 'Don't your mother tell you not to leave the yard?'

I arrived at a very key moment in the funeral proceedings. It was near the beginning and it was nearly the ending as Vavan chopped Hugh Lawrence Brown (for some reason everybody called this boy all of his entire name all the time) in a dispute over who was to carry the coffin. It was a tiny wound really and we persuaded Hugh Lawrence Brown not to go and tell his mother. We had to bribe him by breaking the rules and giving him a whole bulla cake for himself. He ate it right there at the start of the funeral and Harry proceeded to make a bitter remark about 'hungry belly children who just come to nyam off people food'. Apart from these set-backs, the procession went as planned. We lowered the doll into the grave and heaped up a mound of dirt over the hole. We then stuck a cross made from two fudgesticks wired together with an elastic band at the head of the grave and we attempted to sing 'Abide with me', but nobody knew all the words, so we sang instead 'Flow gently sweet Afton', which we had all learned at school. I read Psalm 1 rather badly and too loudly because I was afraid of the rats and of the wrath of my mother, who must have found out that I was missing by now. Even as I read, I imagined myself beneath the ground in a simple wooden box because my mother was surely going to kill me when I went home. She didn't. My father almost did. He whom I loved so much because he was never cross with me. It was the worst beating I ever received, not that he beat me badly, but to be beaten by somebody you loved so much was so humiliating. He said he had to, because I had been 'wilfully disobedient'. He forbade me to visit Bev's house for at least two weeks, and by the end of the two weeks school had started again and Bev got herself a boyfriend and told me I was a child and she couldn't play with me anymore. But I never did hear of anybody else having a Dolly Funeral, so I'm glad I went, no matter what, so there.

I Come Through

One night out at Inn on the Ocean. When I finish singing 'I come through', the place was just quiet, quiet. When I finish singing. All you could hear was the waves slapping against the concrete wall and it was like everybody in the place stopped breathing when I sing 'I come through'.

'When I nearly reach the bottom
Satan call to me and say,
you know I want you for my woman
you know you going to be mine today.
But I hold on to the promise
that my pain is only for a time.
I say, 'back wey satan not me,
no, not this time'.
I rise up like new
I come over, I give thanks,
I come through.'

It take a little while before the people start to clap, and then them clap like them would never stop. Clap till them almost drown out the sound of the sea ... and some of the women and the barmaid was crying. You think is a easy thing to be a woman and a singer in this recording business? If the big, big man star them can get rob, much less a woman who don't have nobody to protect her interest like me.

I could tell you some things! Producer who you have to pay with everything you have before you can go into the studio; disc jockey who want to play with you so your record can get a airplay.

The public who feel that everything you do is their business, if you ever hear some of the things that some total stranger come up to you and ask you because them buy one of you record one time!

I can sing. If is one thing that I can do, I can sing. I sing
big. I like big singing. You know how some people sing a
song like them mean with it, like them swallow part of it
and keep it for themself and then them lend you the rest?
Not me. When I sing, I give everything. Some time when I
finish singing is like I going to dead... it's like I give the
audience my blood. But I don't know any other way...
sometimes I think that one day I'm going to sing a song and
then die right after that.

I have no luck with man. None. Most man don't like their
women to be 'stars'. They love you for it, but they hate you
because of it. I have no luck with man. But I love the same
way I sing, completely, with everything that happen (although
I could never say that I don't regret nothing). I can't regret
really how I stay... what I have in me is like a waterfall... it
just pour out itself from a high place and plenty time it get
beat up on the rocks below... but it still pouring and maybe
one day if I lucky, it will have caught somewhere and settle
nice and peaceful in a pool of water, full of little fish and
delicate waving water-flowers and anybody who weary could
come and just rest themself right there.

The first man I love is the same man who tell me I could
sing and him say would be my producer. Before I record
any song though, I have a baby for him and then another one
and then him start to treat me very bad. Sometimes I used to
wonder if this man get a calling to come and mad me. One
night him put me and the little boy out in the rain... is a good
thing the baby was with my mother. Him put me and the little
boy out in the rain and sey I must go and catch man, for him
spend all him money produce record with me and the record
don't sell and me was of no use to him. When I stand up
outside inna the rain I never exactly curse God but I had to
ask him some hard questions, 'Is what I do so?' 'What make
me salt so?' I give this man everything, all some thing that I
never know I have, I find them and give him and all I getting
is beating and shame. If it wasn't for me son, maybe I woulda

do something to myself that night...but when I start to listen to the devil telling me to 'done it'...I hear my boy say, 'Mamma liff me up'...and so I liff him up...is so I get liff too.

And like a spite, is like from I begin my life with that kind of bad treatment, is like it follow me. Everyman I meet turn out to be another one who come to mad me...is a wonder I never really and truly mad because believe me, I come close, close, close. The last man I was along with before my life change was a man who follow me fi months. That time I never have nobody.

I say I done with man. And this man follow me up and down every time I go to sing somewhere, him was there in front row in the centre a watch me. And him write me and him send message to me by all manner of everybody who know me...just give him a chance no? Finally I give in to him. I get pregnant...somehow is like they don't make a birth control yet that agree with my system. I get pregnant and this same man who follow me and beg me just to give him a chance, him look pon me and ask me if is fi him? You know I never answer him. And I never have the baby. And I write a song about it: 'Little bird, just take flight, be one now with the night. One day when I fly past pain, you and me we'll sing together again.'

Every time I take a beating I write a song (I have a lot of song). My grandmother always say that God have our tears in a bottle...my bottle must be demijohn. You know what a man tell me one time? Him say, 'You must make me feel guilty because I can't live up to you. I feel really bad when I do you the smallest little thing.' But I said, 'I am a human being and I know I have my bad ways too.' I don't expect that two people living together not going to have problems...him say yes...but I can't take the responsibility of hurting you – it make me feel bad, so bad that sometime I just want you to think the worse of me and leave me because I can't live up to you.

95

Another one say...My feelings come in like a baby mole...him fraid to do anything to hurt it so him rather leave it alone. The baby mole, that soft tender place at the top of a little baby's head. Mothers cover it and protect it...who was to cover me? I try to make myself tough one time. But I never get any songs. I try to 'use' people, to talk like a bad woman but I get use more than ever and is like some people just like to hear when I gwan like a bad woman...is like I was giving them a big joke. I work it out that I couldn't really change myself by myself but I was really trying to find a balance.

Then one night I get a vision. I dream that I see a woman at the foot of a hill, her head was pointing down and her two legs were pointing up the hill. When I look around I see that her head was resting in a pile of stinking garbage...a whole heap of rotten stinking rubbish. I could smell it...it was like the garbage of everybody in the world that she was lying down in, it was so rotten and so plenty...and then around her now was a ring of mawgre dog...the dog dem with dem ribs look like scrubbing board and them just a hanker round her and the garbage but mostly them was hankering after her...is like them was waiting for her to dead, with her head inna the garbage. And is like a flash reach me...like I see myself...say it was really me lying down there, for me life was little more than a pile of stinking dirty garbage. I owe money, a mad woman was sending a gunman to me say me take away her man...everytime I cut a song them play it two time on the radio and stop...mi children was not getting proper food...old nyaga was washing them mouth pan me more than ever...my name was at the top of the agenda at every meeting in J. P.'s hairdressing parlour, where barracudas gather to wash their hair and wash their mouth on other women. Them (old nyaga) say me done with, 'She mash up you see!' and mi friend them. My granny always sey when you dream see dog it mean friend. Well my 'friend' them was some mawgre dog! And I remember something else she used to say again...some time when life look like it out fi tumble down pan her and mash her up, she say, 'Lord, make a way,' and I say it. In mi dream I say, 'Lord make a way,' and in the dream it was like a way open in the garbage, and I find a strength and I kick we some of it myself and I find stone and I fling it after the mawgre dog them and them scatter. And I find myself standing up and when I look to my right, I see a big clean pool of water. It look like nobody ever bathe in there yet. It look blue like if God did wear a ring that would be the colour of the stone in the ring. And I take off all my clothes and I bathe and I bathe and I bathe. I wash out my clothes and I spread them on the grass to dry and I bathe till night come and then the moon come up a big round face moon and me did feel like it was all my moon, because my face round too. And the moon bring a lot of stars and she dress up the sky with them and I get all the light that I need to walk up the hill.

See hear. When I wake, I was crying. I was crying so till I feel like I was really in a pool.

Heed your dreams you hear. I couldn't want a plainer dream than that. I get up and I bathe and dress and I beg my mother to keep me children and I take a bus to the country where my grandmother bury and I find her grave and I spend the most part of one whole day sitting down on the tomb and I tell her everything and I say I want me life to change ... gran gran, help me with the mawgre dog and the rubbish I am in ... help me.

And is like I hear her saying ... stop sing for a time, take back your pearls from before the swine and come out of the world until you can go back into the world.

Seven years I live in country. I plant my granny field. I build up back her little house and me and the pickney them fit into the community. Nobody never know me down there as no singer ... them just know me as my grandmother favourite grand-daughter. And them just accept me and help me and laugh and quarrel and cry with me and you want to know sey right before my granny house there was a hill look like the hill in mi dream, and yes there is a pool.

Them say I come late...'where she was all the time?' 'Mi did think she dead.' Plenty of the young people dem never know me...'you ever hear a singer name...(me)?' By this time my boy turn man and him also turn mi manager. What I learn in seven years...what I learn in the seven years I come out of the world so that I could come back for my fullness within the world...what I learn can hold under the cover of one word...LOVE. That is a subject that can take a lifetime to study and you will probably never done. For love is a light that have to catch in you first. And then I will tell you about it in my songs. That's another thing...when I was out of the world I get a new kind of song and a new kind of singing. If you hear me and you knew me before, maybe you might not know me now. I still sing big but now singing uplifts me. I don't want to dead when I finish. Some people say I know things. I know one thing. I come through.

I Don't Want to Go Home in the Dark

He said on the telephone, 'I'm coming to get you.' He had arrived about forty-five minutes later, in his Quink-ink coloured, high-powered German vehicle. He was dressed in a light flannel shirt, designer jeans and very expensive-looking sneakers. He was a big man, with a moustache; he had a latin-lover look like an old-time movie star. He was very handsome. She thought him too handsome. He said, 'I told you I was coming to get you...bring a wrap or a jacket, we're going for a drive up into the hills.'

She liked going up into the hills...the higher you climbed, the more the vegetation became interesting: all sorts of temperate-looking flowers in muted colours, feathery inflorescence and insects not seen below where it was too hot for them to live. Once she'd been buzzed by an iridescent green bug with cellophane-like wings piped in darker green so the wings looked like window panes. Driving up into the hills it got cooler the higher you went, and you could almost imagine you were going for a drive in some foreign country...like you were in a novel, '...and towards evening they drove into an inn for supper'.

Once they were seated in the big car with the real-leather upholstered seats, he began to talk. He talked as if he had stored up everything he had to tell her for a long time, like he was just waiting to see her, to press his release button...she realized that all she had to do was to sit there and maybe say mmmmm every now and again.

Once she realized this, she did what she could do so very well. She slipped out of herself and hoisted herself up on to the roof of the car. It was a great advance view from up there. She could see way ahead of him into the oncoming distance, see the scoops in the road...the rises approaching and into the rooms

of houses; also the wind filled her hair like many whispers and
she laughed out loud and rolled from side to side every time
the car dipped into a hollow. She thought about sitting right
up on the bonnet, right where the silver emblem rode flagship
on the front of the bonnet...it was at best a peace symbol
within a circle, but peace should go with freedom and ought
not be contained in a circle. She decided she was better off
upon the roof. Eventually it was time to go back into herself, so
she wiggled carefully through the window and re-entered, just
in time, for he said just then...finally... 'So how have you
been?' She smiled. He took that for an answer and then he
continued. 'Anyway, there is a farm up ahead, I've put in two
hundred acres and I'm hoping to buy eighty more.' The big
car cleared the gateway and hummed to a stop inside the yard.
There were about ten men standing in the driveway waiting for
him. They all greeted him by crowding around the car and
repeating his name over and over. She watched him turn into
'Landowner' right before her eyes...a big landowner. He used
a different tone when he spoke to the workers. He was firm and
authoritative and was something of a bully. He didn't introduce her, and she stood slightly apart from him wondering
what to do with herself. She decided to sit on an ornate white
garden bench out in the yard and from there to slip out of
herself and go walking around the garden. She turned the
corner away from where he was asking the workers about the
progress of the money trees. 'How many notebuds did you put
in?' 'Did they get enough water?' 'No I don't think that is a
good enough answer.' She noticed a pregnant cat lying on its
side under an azalea bush. The cat was resting like a fallen-
from-grace beauty queen...her belly high with kittens. It was
a touching and lovely sight but what was more exciting was
that the azalea bush, shading the cat, was not alone.

It was part of a whole hedge. As a matter of fact, the entire
yard was bordered by azalea bushes. Can you imagine how
glorious that was going to be when they bloomed? There are
few things lovelier than azaleas in a clay pot shimmering. He

couldn't be so bad after all if he had the good taste to have a yard bordered by azaleas.

She felt that it was time to return. She was right, for as she got back to herself he said, 'It's a good thing you are such a dreamer...you can wait for long periods of time on other people while you dream.' She smiled. He said, 'Come let's go into the house.' She followed him as he took her on a tour of a house which was decorated just right (for some people). But she kept looking around for some spare love lying accidentally somewhere, a kiss left languidly on a smooth surface. Some spare love. She didn't see any. And then there was this magnificent candle holder containing clean candles. And she couldn't help herself, she said, 'I like candles which have burnt...you know? Candles with dripped wings at the sides.' He said, 'What?'

They sit in the living-room, there is a fireplace and she sits close to it...her seat is also near the door.

He sits or rather half-lies across a couch, the upholstery of which complements his shirt very well and he just looks very handsome, half-lying on that couch. Then he speaks...he gives her warning that he is about to speak and then he says, 'Please don't say anything until I have finished.' So she lets him speak. He explains that he finds himself thinking about her a lot at the most inconvenient times and things she says linger in his mind long after she has said them. The truth is he doesn't really have much time in his life for 'something like this' but he wants it. He is an important person, he can afford a lot of things: take this money farm for example, he plans to buy eighty acres of the land adjoining and put in more and more cash suckers and notebuds. She looks sleepy. He quickly says, 'Anyway you get the point of what I'm saying.' He says he knows he can't buy something like what he feels with her...for her... He knows, but right now, is there anything that she needs? Can he get her anything? And she says, 'Yes, azaleas.' And he says, 'What do you mean, azaleas?' And she says, 'Do you know that your whole yard is bordered by an azalea hedge? That's wonderful! And maybe when they bloom, you could bring me some azaleas, you know...like a lot of them. Maybe?'

He said, 'What the hell do you mean? I'm trying to be serious, can't you be serious just once. You drive a ten-year-old car and you live in a flat which is very charming but you don't own it and it might fall on your head soon and you are asking me for azaleas?'

She says, 'Yes.'

He gets really angry. He says, 'I always get what I want, you know.' She says, 'You probably do. Now can you take me home? I don't want to go home in the dark.'

On the way down, he drives very fast so she thinks it's not wise to go outside and sit on the bonnet, he turns the radio on and they are playing some really anonymous music. Usually she can identify songs like ten songs back after they've been played, this time she can't remember which song went before the white bread type one that was now playing. He doesn't speak.

She had hoped he would have stopped and cut some of the temperate looking flowers for her to take home. He does not. She thinks maybe she will just go home and bathe with a soap called *Wild Flowers*...it smelled exactly like mountain flowers and it would balance out the smell of the notebuds and his anger.

The King of Swords

How skilled that man is with a sword. How expertly he inflicts a wound of a word at a time when you are most vulnerable and unsuspecting. Like one night you are all dressed to go out and because the budget is tight and you have not had anything new for a while, you have done your best with everything but your shoes, which are looking a little tired. And his eyes sweep you up and down and he says nothing about your hair (which everyone admires) or your slim figure (from overwork) but comes down on your shoes and mutters, '...those shoes...' so you spend the rest of the night hiding your feet; so he asks you loudly, 'What's wrong with your feet?'

I finally figured out who he reminds me of: 'Aunt B'. He'd die if he heard that. He fancies himself as a very masculine man. But he does remind me of Aunt. They both have eyes which are cold and sharp like a hen's, and they both seem unable to live peacefully with other people...unable to live peacefully inside themselves so they must always be hacking at everyone around them. It's as if they are terrified of what they will find if they sit quietly with themselves...so they live on others.

I am ten years old. I am filled with life. I like to jump up and down on the same spot and skip rope till my calves hurt or just run for ever like horses do.

I should have been a country child...you can't run very far in the city...still I like to run...around and around the play-field at school, to the shop to buy bread and back...I'm always going somewhere very fast. People say, 'This little girl fiery eh?' and Aunt says, 'She is wicked and bad, it's because you don't know her.' There is something which Aunt sees in me as very, very bad and wicked...this thing is contained in my appearance. It's in my eyes which they say are bright...and my smile which appears quickly and my body (I'm small and thin for my age), but sometimes I feel like electric currents are moving in waves through my body...sometimes I feel like I could fly...and sometimes I dream I am floating in the air...above the streets...above the gully with the dead dogs and the unemployed men sitting on the bridge and the people selling fruits and cigarettes and sweeties...above Lola and Violet who sell their bodies on Thursday which is Ben Johnson day and things are really tight...no food in the house then. And I have 'the eye'...I'm always seeing things that nobody else sees. I once heard Aunt (she is not really my aunt, I just call her that). I once heard her telling one of her friends about me and the brother of one of my friends. He was at least twenty, I was ten almost eleven...she said, 'He looks at her the way a big man looks at a big woman, and she so bold, she just look right back into him face.' That was not true, I never could look him in the face because I was terrified of what I saw there.

She saw me looking at her when she spoke, and she shot me a glance of such venom that I immediately crossed my arms over my chest. It was as if I had to protect my heart and the small swellings which were growing on my chest. When she looked at me like that, I always felt wicked and dirty. I already knew I was not as clean as my brother...she had screamed at me one day not to use the same towel as him; she also washed the men's and the women's clothes separately.

I lived with Aunt...because my parents were in England. One day soon they were going to send for me. Occasionally they would send me parcels with pretty clothes. When I dressed up in them, I seemed to incur her wrath even more. She would say things about 'rendering your heart and not your garments' as I went off to church. It seems to me now, that I hardly ever left her presence without carrying away words of disapproval...I was always trying to do something to please her, like make her cups of tea when she had gas pains; she would take the tea and then say, 'It's a pity you are so rude.' I took these remarks into me, right into my ten-year-old heart and I knew from then that I was undeserving of love, that the real me was very wicked and very bad. It occurred to me much later that maybe this woman was practising a strange kind of reverse psychology on me.

She had been very beautiful in her time. She must have been attractive to many men. Maybe she was hoping that if she told me I was bad enough times, I would want to be 'good'. It was the same thing that made people say that a baby was 'ugly' when it was really pretty, because that way you would fool the bad spirits which want to follow beauty, also, to say that a thing was pretty was somehow boasting, and the proud get cut down. But, you see, I had this great need for things to be true. I took her words for their obvious meaning.

I never ever back-answered this woman, not ever. I had worked it out that one day soon my parents were going to send for me to go to England and join them. I was going to go on the boat my mother went on. You see, my father had gone first and then he had written to say that my mother should come. She didn't want to leave us, but the money was not enough for me, my brother and her. So she would go and work some money and send for us. The day she was leaving, I tried to be brave. I went on the boat with her, it was called the *Sea Change*...it looked so shiny and clean and pretty. I wanted with my whole heart to be going with my mother on this shining ship to the faraway land where people claimed it was so cold you had to wear as many as five sweaters at a time and when you spoke, steam came out of your mouth. Then my mother just held me and my brother really tight and asked God to protect us till we could all be together again.

I didn't cry because my brother was crying so much I had to hold him. She told me to have manners to this woman, as she knew I was fiery and I took her charge seriously. So I never answer her back, not one time until that time.

I was always thinking of ways to please this woman, whom I called Aunt to make her like me. And this day, Sunday, I decided to wash up the dishes after dinner, although she didn't ask me. We had visitors after church, so she used her good plates, actually they were plates my mother had sent for us. I was washing them up by the cistern...when I started to think about my mother and father...and as I soaped the plate it was like I could see my mother's face in the plate. My mother's face is very kind...she smiles a lot, she is very gentle. She calls me 'little one'...she laughs at my antics...when people say I'm 'maddy, maddy', my mother says, 'Leave her, I was just like that.' She must have grown very differently though, because now she wasn't 'maddy, maddy'. She was so calm and peaceful...most times. I began to cry and my mother's face dissolved into tears too and slipped away from me and out of my hands and the plate crashed into the cistern. Aunt screamed at me from upstairs. She said that my mind was divided. That is why I could not concentrate.

She said I thought I was a big woman and who had told me to wash her dishes anyway. And that day I answered her. I told her that she had a nasty mind, that she was always telling me what was really in her mind and that it was my mother who had sent the plates anyway. She ran downstairs...and screamed at me that I was dead to trespasses and sins. And I screamed, 'So are you, you old hige. It's like you want to suck my blood, you don't make me prosper. You are an old hige, you need my blood so that you can live.' I've identified her! All the people in the yard heard. From that day on, she hardly said one word, good or bad to me...she also wrote my mother and told her to take me out of her house. That was a blessing, my mother found the money and sent for me and my brother soon after. Aunt's decline was very rapid...it seems that she took sick a few days after we left for England and for the rest of her long life, something was always wrong with her. Many times I thought, 'I should not have answered her.' I *was* dead to trespasses and sin.

I have a history of loving men who cannot love me. I thought anybody who showed an interest in me, loved me. I badly wanted to be good, for somebody to love me because I was good.

I have put up with much from this man, his bullying, his meanness, his insistence on violating everyone around him, his hatred of himself which he transfers to others. I accept it, I accept it all because in a way I am too ashamed to admit to the world that I have chosen badly once again; from afar he looked so good, so kind. Then one afternoon we are talking, or rather he is talking and I am listening, listening to him make great detailed plans for our lives. He has several plans, he has written them out, budgeted the days of our future together. We will spend thirteen days in this place some two years from now ... fifteen nights in this other place and a month doing this or that ... and I listen to him and I wonder how in the world can anybody be so sure of time, so in control of the future. I ask him this and he informs me that he has plans b. and c. in case plan a. does not work and in spite of myself I laugh ... I laugh because I come from a way of life where people always qualify the future ... my mother will say to her sister, I will see you tomorrow ... God willing ... or I will go out next week if life spare. I tell him this and he laughs, he says ... he believes in the Power of the Will ... his will. He has a definition of the word written and put up over his desk ... he says his favourite poem is the one which has the line 'I am the master of my fate, I am the captain of my soul.' I tell him that I read somewhere that the man who wrote those words, lived to regret writing them as fate seemed to single him out particularly for some crippling blows and that he came to realize he had no control over his fate after all. I said I prefer the last line of Robert Frost's 'Goodbye and keep cold': '... Some things have to be left to God.'

He roars when I mention God's name and I can see he is very angry because I am arguing with him ... he becomes very cruel when he is crossed and something tells me he is about to do something to show me this. He gets up and goes over to a drawer and he takes from it a letter I have written to him. In the same way I was always trying to please Aunt, I am always trying to please this man; one of the ways I thought I could do this was by writing him a letter telling him about my deepest fears, about the really personal things which I had told no one about me. I ended the letter by saying I want to show you myself as I really am inside, something I've never shown to anybody. And he takes this gift and he stands in the centre of the room and he reads it out loud, in a mocking, cruel voice, he reads back all my fears and confessions to me ... and he ends his recital by saying, that is you ... so how can you tell me what to do? So I answered him back. For this ultimate violation I answer him back and say ... 'You should read what I've been writing recently, they are called "letters of victory", and I'm going to win a great victory over you and her and them.' I'm thinking about the men who couldn't love me or themselves or who loved themselves to a fault. I'm thinking about Aunt. I'm thinking about him. He is livid, he says, 'who is her, who is them?' I say I'm going to win a great victory over all of you, especially you. Just for a second I see her eyes inside his, cold and hard like a hen's and I say I know who you are, old hige trying come back to claim my life again. And you, I say to him, you are the King of Swords. I have identified him ... their hold over me will decline.

Bella Makes Life

He was embarrassed when he saw her coming toward him.
He wished he could have just disappeared into the crowd and
kept going as far away from Norman Manley Airport
as was possible. Bella returning. Bella come back from
New York after a whole year. Bella dressed in some clothes
which make her look like a checker cab. What in God's
name was a big forty-odd-year-old woman who was fat
when she leave Jamaica, and get worse fat since she go to
America, what was this woman doing dressed like this? Bella
was wearing a stretch-to-fit black pants, over that she had
on a big yellow and black checked blouse, on her feet was a
pair of yellow booties, in her hand was a big yellow handbag
and she had on a pair of yellow-framed glasses. See ya Jesus!
Bella no done yet, she had dyed her hair with red oxide and
Jherri curls it till it shine like it grease and spray. Oh Bella
what happen to you? Joseph never ever bother take in her
anklet and her big bracelets and her gold chain with a
pendant, big as a name plate on a lawyer's office, marked
'Material Girl'.

Joseph could sense the change in Bella through her letters.
When she just went to New York, she used to write him DV
every week.

Dear Joe Joe,

*How keeping my darling? I hope fine. I miss you and the children
so till I think I want to die. Down in Brooklyn here where I'm living,
I see a lot of Jamaicans, but I don't mix up with them. The lady
who sponsor me say that a lot of the Jamaicans up here is doing
wrongs and I don't want to mix up with those things as you can imagine.
You know that I am only here to work some dollars to help you and me to
make life when I come home. Please don't have any other woman while
I'm gone. I know that a man is different from a woman, but please do*

109

try and keep yourself to yourself till we meet and I'm saving all my love for you.

Your sweet, sweet,

Bella

That was one of the first letter that Bella write Joseph, here one of the last letters.

Dear Joseph,

What you saying? I really sorry that my letter take so long to reach you and that the Post Office seem to be robbing people money left, right and centre. Man, Jamaica is something else again. I don't write as often as I used to because I working two jobs. My night job is doing waitressing in a night club on Nostrand Avenue, the work is hard but tips is good. I make friends with a girl on the job named Yvonne and sometimes she and I go with some other friends on a picnic or so up to Bear Mountain. I guess that's where Peaches says she saw me. I figure I might as well enjoy myself while I not so old yet.

Your baby,

Bella

Enjoy herself? This time Joseph was working so hard to send the two children to school clean and neat, Joseph become mother and father for them, even learn to plait the little girl hair. Enjoy himself? Joseph friend them start to laugh after him because is like him done with woman.

Joseph really try to keep himself to himself. Although the nice, nice woman who live at the corner of the next road. Nice woman you know, always talking so pleasant to him. Joseph make sure that the two of them just remain social friends...and Bella up in New York about she gone a Bear Mountain, make blabbamouth Peaches come back from New York and tell everybody in the yard how she buck up Bella a picnic and how Bella really into the Yankee life fully.

It was Norman, Joseph's brother, who said that Bella looked like a checker cab. Norman had driven Joseph and the children to the airport in his van to meet Bella, because she write to say she was coming with a lot of things. When the children saw her they jumped up and down yelling mama come, mama come... When Norman saw her (he was famous for his wit), he said, 'Blerd Naught, a Bella dat, whatta way she favour a checker cab.' When Bella finally cleared her many and huge bags from Customs and come outside, Joseph was very quiet, he didn't know quite how to greet the new Bella. Mark you Bella was always 'nuff' but she really was never as wild as this. She ran up to Joseph and put her arms around him. Part of him felt a great sense of relief that she was home, that Joseph and Bella and their two children were a family once more.

Bella was talking a little too loudly, 'Man, I tell you those customs people really give me a warm time, oh it's so great to be home though, it was so cold in New York!' As she said this she handed her winter coat with its mock fur collar to her daughter who staggered under the weight of it. Norman, who was still chuckling to himself over his checker cab joke, said, 'Bwoy, Bella a you broader than Broadway.' Bella said, 'Tell me about it...'

They all went home. Joseph kind of kept quiet all the way home and allowed the children to be united with their mother... she was still Mama Bella though, asking them about school, if they had received certain parcels she had sent and raising an alarm how she had sent a pair of the latest high-top sneakers for the boy and that they had obviously stolen them at the Post Office.

Every now and again she leaned across and kissed Joseph. He was a little embarrassed but pleased. One time she whispered in his ear, 'I hope you remember I've been saving all my love for you.' This was a new Bella though, the boldness and the forwardness was not the old Bella who used to save all her love for when they were alone together with the bolt on the door.

She would not encourage too much display of affection before the children. That change in Bella pleased Joseph. There were some other changes in Bella that did not please him so much though. Like he thought that all the things in the many suitcases were for their family. No sir! While Bella brought quite a few things for them, she had also brought a lot of things to sell and many evenings when Joe Joe come home from work just wanting a little peace and quiet, to eat his dinner, watch a little TV and go to him bed and hug up his woman, his woman (Bella) was out selling clothes and 'things'. She would go to different offices and apartment buildings and she was always talking about which big important brown girl owed her money... Joseph never loved that. He liked the idea of having extra money, they now had a number of things they could not afford before, but he missed the old Bella who he could just sit down and reason with and talk about certain little things that a one have store up in a one heart... Bella said, America teach her that if you want it, you have to go for it. Joe Joe nearly ask her if she want what? The truth is that Joe Joe felt that they were doing quite all right. He owned a taxi which usually did quite well, they lived in a Government Scheme which gave you the shell of a house on a little piece of land under a scheme called 'Start to build up your own home'... and they had built up quite a comfortable little two-bedroom house with a nice living-room, kitchen, bathroom and verandah. What did Bella mean when she said, 'You have to make it'? As far as Joe Joe was concerned, he had made it. And him was not going to go and kill himself to get to live upon Beverley Hills because anyhow the people up there see all him taxi friend them drive up that way to visit him, them would call police and set guard dog on them... Joe Joe was fairly contented... is what happen to Bella?

'Come ya little Bella, siddown, make me ask you something. You no think say that you could just park the buying and selling little make me and you reason bout somethings?'

'Joe Joe, you live well yah. I have three girls from the bank coming to fit some dresses and if them buy them then is good breads that.'

After a while, Joe Joe stopped trying to reclaim their friendship. After a month, Bella said she wanted to go back to New York. Joe Joe asked her if she was serious.

'You know that nobody can't love you like me, Joe Joe.'

Joe Joe wondered about that. Sometimes he looked at the lady at the corner of the next road, their social friendship had been severely curtailed since Bella returned home, but sometimes he found himself missing the little talks they used to have about life and things in general.

She was a very simple woman. He liked her style, she was not fussy. Sometimes he noticed a man coming to her, the man drive a Lada, look like him could work with the Government, but him look married too. You know how some man just look married? Well this man here look like a man who wear a plaid bermuda shorts with slippers when him relax on a Sunday evening, and that is a married man uniform.

When Joe Joe begun to think of life without Bella, the lady at the corner of the next road began to look better and better to him.

'So Bella really gone back a New York?'

'Yes mi dear, she say she got to make it while she can.'

'Make what?'

'It!'

'A wha it so?'

'You know . . . Oh forget it.'

And that is what Joe Joe decided to do. The lady, whose name was Miss Blossom, started to send over dinner for Joe Joe not long after Bella went back to New York.

'Be careful of them stew peas and rice you a eat from that lady they you know, mine she want tie you.' Joe Joe said, 'True?' and continued eating the dinner that Miss Blossom had sent over for him. He didn't care what Peaches said, her mouth was too big anyway. He just wanted to enjoy eating the 'woman food'. Somehow, food taste different, taste more nourishing when a woman cook it.

Bella write to say that she was doing fine.

Dear Joe Joe,

I know you're mad with me because you didn't want me to come back to the States, but darling, I'm just trying to make it so that you and me and the children can live a better life and stop having to box feeding outta hog mouth.

Now that really hurt Joe Joe. He would never describe their life together as that... True, sometimes things had been tight but they always had enough to eat and wear. Box feeding outta hog mouth... that was the lowest level of human existence and all these years he thought they were doing fine, that is how Bella saw their life together... well sir. Joe Joe was so vex that him never even bother to reply to that letter.

Joe Joe started to take Miss Blossom to pictures and little by little the line of demarcation between social friends and sweetheart just blurred. Joe Joe tell her that the married man better stop come to her and Miss Blossom say him was only a social friend and Joe Joe say 'Yes', just like how him and her was social friend... and she told him he was too jealous and him say yes he was, 'But I don't want to see the man in here again,' and she said, 'Lord, Joe Joe.'

Little by little Miss Blossom started to look after the children and look after Joe Joe clothes and meals, is like they choose to forget Bella altogether. Then one Christmas time Bella phone over the grocery shop and tell Mr Lee to tell Joe Joe that she was coming home for Christmas.

Well to tell the truth, Joe Joe never want to hear anything like that. Although Miss Blossom couldn't compare to Bella because Bella was the first woman Joe Joe ever really love... Joe Joe was feeling quite contented and he was a simple man, him never really want to take on Bella and her excitement and her 'got to make it'. Anyway, him tell Miss Blossom say Bella coming home and she say to him, 'Well Joe, I think you should tell her that anything stay too long will serve two masters, or two mistresses as the case might be.'

Joe Joe say, 'Mmmmm...but remember say Bella is mi baby mother you know and no matter what is the situation, respect is due.'

Miss Blossom said that, 'When Bella take up herself and gone to New York and leave him, she should know that respect was due to him too.' Joe Joe say, 'Yes', but him is a man who believe that all things must be done decently and in good order, so if him was going to put away Bella him would have to do it in the right and proper way. Miss Blossom say she hope that when Bella gone again him don't bother ask her fi nuttin. Joe Joe became very depressed.

If Bella looked like a checker cab the first time, she looked like Miami Vice this time, inna a pants suit that look like it have in every colour flowers in the world and the colour them loud! And Bella broader than ever... Oh man. Norman said, 'Bees mus take up Bella inna that clothes dey. Any how she pass Hope Gardens them must water her.'

Bella seemed to be oblivious to the fact that Joe Joe was under great strain. She greeted him as if they had parted yesterday, 'Joe Joe what you saying sweet pea.' Joe Joe just looked at her and shook his head and said, 'Wha happen Bella?' They went home but Joe Joe felt like he and the children went to meet a stranger at the airport. Bella had become even stranger than before to Joe Joe. He began to wonder exactly what she was doing in America, if she really was just waitressing at that club. Bella told him that he should come forward, because this was the age of women's liberation, and Joe Joe told her that maybe she should liberate her backside outta him life because he couldn't take her.

Bella cried and said how much she loved him. Then things became really intense and it was like a movie and they had to turn up the radio really high to prevent the children from hearing them.

115

Joe Joe decided to just bite him tongue while Bella was home. He took to coming home very late all through the Christmas season because the house was usually full of Bella's posse including the 'Yvonne' of Bear Mountain Fame, and when they came to visit the house was just full up of loud laughing and talking and all kinds of references that Joe Joe didn't understand. The truth was that he was really dying for Bella to leave. He really didn't much like the woman she had become. First of all everything she gave to him or the children, she tell them how much it cost... 'Devon, beg you don't bother to take that Walkman outside, is Twenty-Nine Ninety-Nine, I pay for it at Crazy Eddies,' or, 'Ann-Marie, just take time with that jagging suit, I pay Twenty-Three Dollars for it in May's Department Store. Oh Lord.'

Bella also came armed with two junior Jherri curls kits and one day Joe Joe come home and find him son and him daughter heads well Jherri curls off.

Joe Joe nearly went mad. 'So you want Devon fi tun pimp or what?'

'Joe, you really so behind time, you should see all the kids on my block.'

'On your block, well me ago black up you eye if you don't find some way fi take that nastiness outta my youth man hair, him look like a cocaine seller. Bella what the hell do you, you make America turn you inna idiat? Why you don't just gwan up there and stay then, me tired a you foolishness...'

Bella couldn't believe that Joe Joe was saying this to her...then she told him that he was a worthless good-for-nuttin and that him never have no ambition, him just want to stay right inna the little two by four (their house) and no want no better and that she was really looking for a better way and that he clearly did not fit into her plans.

Joe Joe say him glad she talk what was in her mind because now him realize say that she was really just a use him fi convenience through nobody a New York no want her. Bella said...then he said... Oh, they said some things to each other!

One thing though, Bella catch her fraid and try wash out the Jherri curls outta Devon hair. No amount of washing could bring it round. The barber had was to nearly bald the little boy head and he spent the worse Christmas of his life.

All his friends 'smashed' him as they passed by. As New Year done so, Bella pack up herself and went back to New York.

Joe Joe make a two weeks pass before him make a check by Miss Blossom. The whole Christmas gone him never see her. He figured that she had gone to spend the holidays in the country with her family. When he asked in the yard where she was, they told him they had no idea where she was gone, and that her room was empty. Joe Joe felt like a beaten man. He went home and decided to just look after him two children and just rest within himself. About a month later he was driving home when he saw somebody looking like Miss Blossom standing at the corner of the road. It look like Miss Blossom, but no, it couldn't be, this woman was dressed like a punk...in full black, she had on a black socks with a lace frothing over the top of her black leather ankle boots. A big woman. He slowed the cab down and said, 'Blossom...where you was?'...and then he thought quickly, 'No, don't bother answer me...you go to New York, right?'

'No,' said Blossom, 'I was in Fort Lawdadale. You seem to think only Bella one can go to America.'

Joe Joe never even bother ask her if she want a drive, him just draw a gear and move off down the road, then him go inside him house and slam the door.

Before him drop asleep, it come to him that maybe what him should do was to find an American woman who wanted to live a simple life in Jamaica. Him know a rasta man who have a nice yankee woman like that...

Glossary: reading the text

Maya Angelou

Incident in the Yard

4 *with a smirk that unprofane people can't control when venturing into profanity* with an embarrassed smile because she is talking about private parts of the body.

clabbered milk curdled milk, a drink like yoghurt.

switch thin branch used to beat children.

moccasins and rattlers venomous snakes.

Buhbah affectionate name for an older male ('brother').

appellations names.

powhitetrash 'poor white trash', a derogatory name for the white agricultural workers and share-croppers who were as poor, and often poorer, than black people. They had, nevertheless, the status of being white – they could vote, had rights in law and had social superiority.

5 *apparitions* ghosts.

They called my uncle by his first name this shows great disrespect.

limping dip-straight-dip fashion Uncle Willie had been injured when young.

extry sody crackers more (extra) soda crackers (rather like water biscuits).

roustabout a labourer who could not be expected to know much about good manners.

a cat-o'-nine-tails a whip with nine cords, each with a knot at the end, that was used to beat slaves.

6 ***one of those community pillars***   important people. Mr McElroy is a black man who owns his own house and land – unusual in Stamps.

  Sister   Momma's name for Maya. It shows respect and affection.

  behind the screen door   homes in the Southern states are protected from flying insects by thin mesh screens.

7 ***molasses***   slow. Molasses is a thick dark treacle, very popular in the South. Being viscous, it pours out very slowly.

  pooched out   stuck out – a rude reference to the shape of Momma's lips.

  lye   detergent or bleach.

  dirty scummy peckerwoods   a 'peckerwood' is a poor Southern white. Black people in the South were called blackbirds and ironically called whites red woodpeckers (i.e. with red heads and necks).

8 ***"Bye, Annie' ... "Bye, Miz Helen ...'***   the children do not call Momma by her title, but she calls them 'Miss'.

  A firecracker July-the-Fourth burst   like fireworks exploding on the Fourth of July, which is when Americans celebrate their 1776 Declaration of Independence.

  breasting the hill   coming over the top of the hill.

9 ***touched me as mothers of the church 'lay hands on the sick and afflicted'***   soothed me, as religious women heal people who are sick or unhappy by touching them.

Names

10 ***You were a debutante***   debutantes were young women from the richest and most élite families in British and American society.

  ecru tatting thread   unbleached cotton thread which could be knotted into lacy edges for tablecloths, etc.

  sacheted   containing little bags of sweet-smelling herbs or dried flowers.

11 *Virginia*   a Southern state known for its plantation slavery.

servants' bells   large houses had bells in each room to summon the servants.

sherbet   a cool drink made of fruit-juice and ice.

12 *the doctor had taken out all her lady organs*   she had had her womb removed.

embalmed   preserved – by soaking in alcohol, like fruits.

the Cheshire cat's smile   the Cheshire cat is a character from *Alice in Wonderland.*

straighten their hair   curly African hair was not thought to be beautiful at this time, as standards of beauty were determined by whites. In the sixties, the 'Black is beautiful' slogan heralded a change in political thinking and popularised natural-look hairstyles, such as the Afro and 'Soul' look.

braids   plaits.

She doesn't talk much   Maya was mute at this point in her life, as a result of the shock of having been raped by her mother's boyfriend, Mr Freeman.

13 *couldn't even pronounce my name correctly*   Maya's real name was Marguerite (with the accent on the last syllable). Mrs Cullinan had called her Margaret.

I'd call her Mary if I was you   even in the 1930s it was common practice for white people to re-name their black servants to suit themselves – a re-definition which black people bitterly resented as a reminder of slavery.

four o' clocks   daisy-like flowers that closed their petals at four o' clock.

14 *'called out of his name'*   being called anything other than his own name. The list which follows is a catalogue of the insulting terms commonly used to refer to black people, usually with a reference to their colour.

I looked into Mrs. Cullinan's face   among the black community, it was regarded as very rude for a child to look an adult in the face.

15 **shards**   broken pieces of pottery.

Visit to the Dentist

17 **the Angel of the candy counter had found me out at last**   in Christianity, the Recording Angel knows all that a person has done and weighs sins against good deeds before deciding whether s/he may enter heaven or must be given a penance (punishment). Maya has done wrong (taking sweets from the Store). The 'excruciating penance' means she has holes (cavities) in her teeth and extremely bad toothache as a punishment for her wrongdoing.

beyond the bailiwick of crushed aspirin or oil of cloves beyond the control of the usual cures for toothache.

he owed her a favor   during the Depression the economy of the USA collapsed, leaving many people out of work and desperate. Momma had been generous in lending money and help.

18 **Listerine**   antiseptic mouthwash.

the jarring of my molars dislodged what little remained of my reason   the vibration of cleaning her teeth made Maya feel she was going mad with pain.

an aura that haloed me for three feet around   Maya seemed to be at the centre of a circle of pain.

calaboose   prison.

19 **as if she had no last name**   the way a person is addressed is important. Slaves had no family names, unless they were given their masters' names. In the black community Momma would always be known as Mrs Henderson or Sister Henderson. In the white community for her to be called anything but Annie would suggest that she was as worthy of respect as a white person.

20 **Momma walked in that room as if she owned it**   the part of

the story in italics is what Maya imagines might be happening inside Dentist Lincoln's office.

21 **R.O.T.C.** Reserve Officer Training Corps.

Sorry is as sorry does saying sorry is easy; your actions will show whether you are really sorry.

and you're about the sorriest dentist I ever laid my eyes on this is a pun on 'sorriest' meaning 'most sorry for what he has done' and also 'most weak and weedy'.

vernacular language of the people.

epizootic a disease caused by parasites that live on the body of another animal.

varlet bad servant – an old-fashioned word.

a crocus sack a hessian sack used for storing vegetables, grain, animal feed etc.

22 **Mum** deodorant.

the Greyhound the Greyhound bus company travels long distances between towns all over America. Momma takes a seat in the back because black people were segregated from whites and not allowed to ride 'up front'.

23 **uppity** arrogant. Ironically, 'uppity' was often used by prejudiced whites against blacks who had been successful.

that little snippity nurse there is no literal translation of this: the sense is conveyed through the sounds of the words rather than their actual meaning. We get a vivid picture from 'snippity' of the prim, tight-mouthed, disapproving young nurse. This use of onomatopoeia is a characteristic of black English whether from the USA, the Caribbean or Britain.

her retributive sin Momma's 'sin' was in demanding money from the man as interest on the loan she made him. Retribution is divine punishment or reward for what has been done, so it is his punishment that he pays for his racism and cruelty, and her reward for her generosity that she gets money out of him to pay for Maya's treatment.

Alice Walker

Nineteen Fifty-Five

Alice Walker has developed this story from real events. In 1952 a black rhythm and blues singer called Willie Mae 'Big Mama' Thornton recorded a song called 'Hound Dog', written by Jerry Lieber and Mike Stoller. She had a powerful voice, an exuberant stage manner and she weighed about 200 pounds. Elvis Presley (Traynor), who was then still in the early stages of his career, heard her version of the song and his manager, Colonel Tom Parker ('the Deacon' in the story) bought the song for $500. Elvis recorded his version, closely copied from Big Mama's, on 2 July 1956 in the New York RCA studio. Although it became an immediate, huge hit, especially in his stage show, Elvis is said never to have liked the song much. The song sold over 2 million copies, but Big Mama never made any more money from it. Big Mama continued her career in rhythm and blues and folk music throughout the 1950s and 1960s and played with many of the great names in folk and blues in jazz festivals into the 1980s. On 25 July 1984 she died of a heart attack in Los Angeles, California.

Details of Elvis Presley's life are incorporated into the story: he made a great number of hit records and some films, was drafted into the US army, was posted to Germany, married and built a huge palatial mansion, Graceland, in Memphis. His marriage broke down, and, although he was still a very successful singer, he gave up stage shows as he had put on a great deal of weight. Elvis Presley died of a heart attack at Graceland in 1977.

26 **brandnew red Thunderbird convertible**   a very expensive American car.

dressed like a Baptist deacon   dressed very plainly in black clothes.

a Loosianna creole   someone from Louisiana of mixed black and white parents.

27 Practically cut his teeth on you   grew up singing your songs from babyhood.

28 colored   a 'polite' term for a black man or woman. 'The deacon' means that a black man would offer Gracie Mae less for her song than he did.

race record shops   shops where black people's music is sold.

And they gonna push all them other records of yourn they got   and they're going to publicise and sell all your other records.

Yankees beat the Orioles 10–6   two teams in the baseball game he had been watching.

little low-life jook   small sleazy night-club or bar with a juke-box where singers could perform (see note on page 123 for details of the life of the 'real' Gracie Mae).

my singing made ... Honey, hush!   Gracie Mae's singing was full of feelings that the men and women recognised and shared.

29 Little Mama   an affectionate name for their large grandmother. The 'real' Gracie Mae was known as 'Big Mama' (see note on page 123).

smash   'Hound Dog' was a big hit for singer Elvis Presley in 1956.

30 bourbon   rye whisky.

complicit   sharing the joke with him.

Grand Ole Opry ... Ed Sullivan show ... Mike Douglas ... the Cotton Bowl ... the Orange Bowl   Grand Ole Opry is a Country and Western road show; the Ed Sullivan Show and Mike Douglas are television and radio shows; the Cotton Bowl and the Orange Bowl are football games – all are famous.

30–1 When you fool around with a lot of no count mens you sing a bunch of 'em   when you've known a lot of worthless men in your life, you put your feelings about your experiences into your songs.

31 making 'miration   admiring it.

the draft   compulsory national service; all young men had to spend some years in the army, airforce, navy or marines.

32 **the womens was on him like white on rice**   the women stuck closely to him.

33 **I can hardly git through 'em without gagging**   the songs are so silly they make him feel sick.

Malcolm X, King, the president and his brother   Malcolm X was a black leader, assassinated in 1965; Dr Martin Luther King Jr was a Civil Rights campaigner and black leader, assassinated in 1968; John F Kennedy was the president of the USA, assassinated in 1963; his brother was Robert Kennedy, a senator and presidential candidate, assassinated in 1968.

Ray Charles   a famous blind black singer with a slow husky voice.

the Klan   the Ku Klux Klan is an organisation of racist white people which began in the Southern states and spread. Members wear white robes and pointed white hoods so that they cannot be identified.

An Arab like the ones you see in storybooks. Plump and soft   Gracie Mae is thinking of the stereotypical (and racist) images of rich Arab sheiks presented in books and films.

34 **That's it for Horace**   that's enough for Horace; he doesn't like being confused with J. T.

35 **Bessie Smith**   a famous blues singer.

chorine   a chorus girl.

to live long enough to put your young bluffs to use   to do the things that you pretended that you did when you were younger.

Them words could hold me up   those words are the truth of my life.

36 **Miss ... Nobody from Notasulga**   Miss Nobody from Nowhere.

37 **The Tara Hotel**   Tara was the splendid Southern mansion in the book and film **Gone with the Wind**.

39 ***One of his flunkies zombies up***   one of his servants comes up silently and without any expression.

    Johnny Carson   a famous TV personality with a very popular show.

    Hard Shell Baptist church   a Southern country Baptist church where singing and shouting was seen as a means of praising the Lord.

39–40 ***Them that waits for programs ... is just good voices occupying body space***   you have to sing a song the way that you feel it should be sung, with emotion, and not just wait for anyone else to tell you how to do it.

40 ***flaky***   wouldn't know good singing from bad.

    my fat is the hurt I don't admit, not even to myself   I am fat because it's a way of hiding myself and not admitting that I'm hurt about the things that have happened in my life.

The Flowers

42 ***smokehouse***   a building where fish and meat were smoked over wood fires to preserve them for the winter.

    squash   a marrow.

    her family's sharecropper cabin   poor people in the South farmed land for a landowner in return for a share of the crop. The landowner also supplied the sharecroppers with a house, often in very poor condition. Sharecroppers could be thrown off the land and out of their home at any time.

    a sweetsuds bush   a plant used to scent the water for washing.

43 ***plowline***   the rope used for tying the plough behind the horse or mule.

    benignly   harmlessly.

To Hell with Dying

44 *Spanish moss* a common plant in the Southern states, which is epiphytic (grows on another plant); often called 'Long-beard' because of its appearance.

fare better are safer (because they are not seen as being 'uppity' by whites).

shiftless lazy and irresponsible.

spent money as if he were trying to see the bottom of the mint was very extravagant – as if he were trying to spend money faster than the mint could print it.

'li'l necessaries' things a person must have in life.

45 *strangely acute* particularly alert.

46 *impenetrable* so thick fingers couldn't go through it.

'Sweet Georgia Brown', 'Caldonia' well-known tunes of the time.

Chi-ca-go, or De-stroy, Michigan spelt this way to reflect the pronunciation; De-stroy is Detroit.

participating in one of Mr. Sweet's 'revivals' taking part in the ritual of bringing Mr Sweet back to life.

rehabilitation being taught to live again.

47 *the crossover* the moment of crossing from life to death.

a ham a bad actor.

implacable death inevitable, irresistible death. This is ironic, since Mr Sweet has avoided 'implacable' death on numerous occasions.

he let me do all the revivaling the whole ritual is described like a theatrical performance.

49 *a trifle contemptuous of people who let themselves be carried away* he began to feel superior to people who could not be brought back to life and simply died.

down-home blues way a particular way of playing and singing blues, common in the South.

doctorate   university degree of Doctor, which is not necessarily a doctor of medicine. Alice Walker became a Doctor of Literature.

51 steel box   the guitar body.

Olive Senior

Love Orange

54 Work out your own salvation with fear and trembling   from St Paul's Epistle to the Philippians (2:12) in the New Testament of the Bible. It is the sort of verse that children learnt and repeated at Sunday School.

talisman   anything that acts as a charm and protects against evil or brings good; for the girl, it is a saying ('our worlds wait outside') which she believes protects her from danger.

Experience can wait ... death too   she is making up a new talisman, which reflects the fact that she hasn't yet found out about 'the worlds outside'.

55 in a moment of rare passion ... but would quickly withdraw my hand each time   the girl means that sometimes, very rarely, she wanted to show the dog or her grandmother that she loved them but was afraid to.

camphor   insect repellent; it smells like mothballs.

allamanda tree   a flowering tree.

56 oblique   indirect.

corseted and whaleboned grandmother ... in a black romaine dress   the grandmother is wearing her best clothes and is strictly bound by tight corsets so that she can get into them.

laid her out   prepared her for burial.

57 a calico skull cap   a close-fitting white cotton cap.

came back only as ashes   he had died and been cremated in England.

Do Angels Wear Brassieres?

This story is written in Jamaican Creole. You will be able to guess at the meaning most of the time but the notes below will help you.

59 *Beccka vex* Beccka was annoyed.

Not praying for nobody that tek weh mi best glassy eye marble I'm not praying for anyone who has taken away my best glass-eye marble.

Imitations of Christ a holy Christian book.

anansi a spider with human (and sometimes superhuman) characteristics, hero of West African folk stories. Anansi is a trickster, and survives by cunning, but he champions the weak against the strong.

Beccka want to try and find flaw and question she can best them with Beccka wants to find ways of tricking those who think they know their Bible so that she can make fools of them.

60 *cotch* live.

Braps! typical Jamaican exclamation conveying dramatic change.

mannersable well-mannered.

pickney child.

hard-back man healthy, strong man.

you no think Cherry buck up the devil own self when she carrying her? don't you think Cherry must have met the devil himself when she was pregnant with Beccka? Folk belief in many cultures says that the unborn child is affected if a pregnant woman meets certain animals or the devil.

she pop one big bawling she started screaming.

61 *Is just hard ears she hard ears* she is just obstinate and disobedient. The repetition is typical of Creole.

Den no so me saying? Isn't that what I'm saying?

by bus' ass pardon my french by beating (excuse my bad language).

force-ripe   precocious; too cheeky and grown up for her age.

'Say what, maam?' ... 'she forget bout worm and reproduction   Auntie Mary and Katie are appalled that Beccka should ask questions to do with sex.

if is lie I lie   if I'm telling a lie.

like autoclaps   just like that.

62 **Bellevue**   famous asylum for the insane.

facety   cheeky, impertinent.

get her comeuppance on Judgement Day   get what she deserves, i.e. be too fat to rise up to heaven with the other Christians.

64 **The Archdeacon is coming**   a major social event for Auntie Mary who is a devout church-member but from the lower class.

a bottle of pimento dram   home-made liqueur from pimentos in rum, which is very strong.

Christmas Curtains   the best curtains, put up for Christmas and special occasions but taken down for the rest of the year.

antimacassars   a covering put over settees and chairs to protect them.

66 **Galatians six eleven**   New Testament: Paul's Epistle to the Galatians, chapter 6, verse 11.

ease him up   ask him an easy one.

'What did Adam and Eve do ...' 'They raised Cain Ho Ho Ho Ho Ho'   the Archdeacon is worried by the question because he is afraid Beccka is referring to sex. 'Raised Cain' means that they brought up their son, Cain, but it also means to create trouble. The Archdeacon and Beccka go on asking questions, the answers to which are all verses from the Bible but misinterpreted deliberately.

67 **being prepared for confirmation**   learning the Bible in order to make promises to confirm her as a Christian in a special ceremony.

68 ***the poor child dont have no father to speak of*** Beccka's
father is no use to her financially.

   please like puss delighted (c.f. 'like the cat that got the cream').

   vain like peacock in ribbons and clothes Beccka loves ribbons
   and clothes and anything new and is very vain about her
   appearance.

   When Beccka think done when she had finished thinking …
   she imagines a life she would prefer to school.

69 ***a yellow nicol*** the yellow seed of a plant, used by children like
   marbles.

   taa a special marble.

   john crow vultures common in Jamaica.

70 ***Is sleep Beccka sleep*** Beccka fell asleep.

   she see a stand above her she saw, standing above her.

   pindar cake sweets made of brown sugar and peanuts.

71 ***Beccka laugh cant done*** Beccka couldn't stop laughing.

The Boy Who Loved Ice Cream

72 ***Harvest Festival Sale*** great social occasions, attracting people
   from all nearby villages and sellers of goods from all over the
   island.

   a 'strainer' a loofah: the fruit of a vine, which is dried so that
   the inside becomes like a net of fibres, used to strain liquids or
   scrub the skin.

   jumbo-head bwoy stupid boy.

   a konk yu till yu fenny I'll hit you (around the head) until
   you're sick.

73 ***an ice cream bucket*** a machine with a handle to churn the ice
   cream.

   a mampala man yu a raise? are you raising a softie?

74 ***Tata Maud*** Auntie Maud – Tata is a name for any older woman.

the drops, the wangla   'drops' are sweets made with coconut and condensed milk; 'wangla' is sugar-cake made with nuts, which was originally made with the seeds of the wangla tree.

serge   a wool fabric used for making men's suits.

Benjy   Benjamin was the youngest of Joseph's brothers and, after Joseph, the favourite of his father, Jacob (Genesis 39–40; 42:1–46:30).

junjo   a name for any kind of fungus or mould.

75 **Kingston**   capital of Jamaica; this story is set in rural Jamaica.

76 **then is jacket**   then the child is not the man's own child; 'jacket' means cuckold.

Jus a wait for Icy finish iron mi frock ... A ketch yu up soon   I'm just waiting for Icy to finish ironing my dress. I'll catch you up soon.

77 **What yu all doing back there a lagga lagga so?**   What are you all doing dawdling back there? ('lagga lagga' for emphasis and 'yu all' for the plural).

Commons   common land: a field owned by the church.

marl   white limestone rock common in rural Jamaica.

abandoning their chaste Sunday white   not wearing their white Sunday dresses.

77–8 **'upstairs' houses with fretwork balconies**   two-storey houses are not very common in rural Jamaica; those there are often have an upstairs verandah.

78 **'Crown and Anchor'**   a gambling game.

79 **drawing the line only ... liquor on the premises**   forbidding only the selling and drinking of alcohol (rum) on church property.

bougainvillea   common and pretty flowering plant

bottle torches   torches of oil or candle, in bottles to protect them from the wind.

Mass Vass   'Mass' or 'Mars' is short for master and shows respect.

80 **Nuh mine ... Papa wi gi wi ice cream. When de time come**
never mind, Papa will give us ice cream when he thinks it is time
for it.

81 **But wa do yu ee bwoy** what's the matter with you, eh, boy?

pone a pudding made of sweet-potato, maize, sugar and
spices.

baad the best (the opposite of what it says).

**A bawl yu wan' bawl? Doan mek I give yu something fe bawl
bout** you want to cry? Don't make me give you something to
cry about (that is, a slap).

82 **the Extension Officer** a government official whose job was to
support and advise small farmers.

83 **grater cake and snowballs** cakes made of grated coconut and
raw brown sugar, and drinks made of shaved ice with sweet
syrup poured over.

84 **paradise plums and jujubs** paradise plums are red and yellow
sweets; jujubs are pastilles.

85 **kitchen bitches** a small lamp made of tin.

tilly lamp a paraffin lamp.

Lorna Goodison

The Dolly Funeral

This story is based on a real incident in Lorna Goodison's childhood.

88 **'their own place' ... a many-roomed yard** they owned their
own yard; everyone else rented a yard or rooms in someone
else's yard. Yard life is an intimate, communal lifestyle, often
with homes on three sides of a square, each containing a
different family.

'sitting down bad' or 'common behaviour'   good manners and knowing how to behave properly ('brought-upsy') are extremely important in Jamaica.

'beyave' ... 'Gweyframme'   behave! ... leave me alone!

tear his backside   beat him ('backside' is rude in Jamaica).

89 **'dead house'**   coffin.

pit latrine   the yard toilet: a little wooden hut around a deep hole.

ackee tree   common tree with edible fruit: ackee and saltfish is a national dish.

90 **bulla cake**   a hard sweet flat cake, popular among children.

belly-wash   a drink made with fresh limes and sugar, but so weak that it is almost like plain water.

I pleaded with her, I enquired of her ... 'just please do, I beg you, mama, make me go'   notice the formality of the Standard language as the child politely begins the pleading and the vernacular of the end; 'make me go' means 'let me go'.

91 **Chuh just teef out**   just sneak out; 'chuh' or 'cho' is an expression of irritation or contempt, 'teef' means 'steal'.

the gully   a deep channel behind the yards for waste water and to cope with floods in the heavy rains; often very dangerous.

'hungry belly children who just come to nyam off people food'   starving children who only came to the funeral so they could eat the food. 'Nyam' (meaning 'eat') is an example of a West African word which has come into Creole.

fudgesticks   wooden lollipop sticks.

I Come Through

93 **back wey**   go away.

who want to play with you so your record can get a airplay   who want sexual favours in return for agreeing to play your record on their radio programmes.

94 *how I stay*   what sort of person I am.

get a calling to come and mad me   was sent by God to drive me mad.

sey I must go and catch man   told me to find another man or, possibly, sell myself as a prostitute.

'Is what I do so?' 'What make me salt so?'   what did I do? What have I done to deserve such suffering?

95 *the devil telling me to 'done it'*   the devil tempting me to kill myself.

And like a spite ... it follow me   and from the time that things began to go wrong in my life, they went on going wrong.

him look pon me and ask me if is fi him   he looked straight at me and asked whether the baby was his.

demijohn   a large bottle with a bulging body.

96 *baby mole*   the vulnerable soft part of a baby's head before the skull hardens. The narrator means that her feelings leave her vulnerable and unprotected.

I gwan like a bad woman   I behave badly.

mawgre   thin, scrawny.

sending a gunman to me say me take away her man   sending a gunman to threaten my life, saying that I had taken her man.

old nyaga was washing them mouth pan me   no-good people were gossiping about me.

barracudas   dangerous fish; the narrator means the local women.

Them (old nyaga) say ... 'She mash up you see!' and mi friend them   the wretches say I'm finished, 'Her career is over!' and they are supposed to be my friends.

when you dream see dog it mean friend   when you dream you see a dog it means something about a friend.

6–7 *when life look like it out fi tumble down pan her and mash her up*   when everything in life seems to be determined to crush her and destroy her. Abstract nouns (e.g. 'life') are humanised (given the power of thought, will and action).

97 kick we   kick away.

take back your pearls from before the swine   a reference to the biblical saying not to cast pearls before swine, i.e. not to waste your talents on those who do not appreciate them.

I plant my granny field   I farmed the land that my grandmother had owned.

the pickney them   the children. The plural is made by adding 'them' to the noun.

98 Them say I come late   they said I made a late come-back.

you ever hear a singer name ... (me)?   have you ever heard of a singer called ... (my name)?

I Don't Want to Go Home in the Dark

99 Quink-ink coloured, high powered German vehicle   dark blue Mercedes Benz.

inflorescence   blossom.

iridescent   shining with the colours of the rainbow.

scoops   holes.

100 where the silver emblem rode flagship ... a peace symbol within a circle   where the silver emblem was placed at the front of the car. The Mercedes symbol is a circle with an upside-down Y in it; it looks a bit like the international peace sign used by the Campaign for Nuclear Disarmament.

money trees ... notebuds   he talks of his money and his land as if he is planting money rather than anything natural which will grow in the earth.

101 cash suckers   young money-shoots (see note above).

102 anonymous music ... the white bread song   the songs all sound alike, as if they have been produced in a factory; they sound as if all the heart and meaning has been taken out of them.

The King of Swords

103 ***The King of Swords*** the sword is a symbol of the way that the man hurts the woman. The King of Swords is also the name of a card in most Tarot packs, where it signifies a person who thinks a great deal and does not have much regard for emotions.

I am ten years old Lorna Goodison moves backwards and forwards in time in this story.

104 ***sell their bodies on Thursday*** as Friday is pay-day, Thursday is the day when money is most limited and the cupboards are bare, so the women make a little money from prostitution to tide them over.

I have 'the eye' I have the power to see things other people do not see.

'rendering your heart and not your garments' in Christianity it is what is in your heart that pleases God, not outward appearances. 'Aunt B' means that it is no good going to church to show off your pretty clothes.

gas pains wind.

105 ***practising a strange kind of reverse psychology on me*** telling me how bad I was so that I would try harder to be good. Lorna Goodison believes that women in the Caribbean brought up their daughters 'hard' like this to toughen them up to face the hardships of life, and that this is a legacy of behaviour from times of slavery.

the proud get cut down a reference to the Bible.

So she would go and work some money and send for us a very common situation in the Caribbean in the fifties, sixties and early seventies: children were left in the care of female relatives (most often grandmothers) while their parents went abroad to work and saved money for the fares to bring the children to join them.

her charge her mother's command.

106 *maddy, maddy* crazy, wild.

she was always telling me what was really in her mind what she said about me was more true of her.

dead to trespasses and sins unable to recognise her own sins; Christians believe that a sinner who repents can be forgiven and saved from hell, but one who will not repent is beyond redemption.

old hige in Jamaican folklore, a witch who can take off her skin and fly at nights, when she sucks the blood of young children. 'Aunt B' is an 'old hige' because she is sucking the life out of the child with her cruel comments.

I've identified her! she has named the witch and so taken some of her power away.

107 *violating* brutally attacking (in words or actions).

budgeted the days of our future together the idea of budgeting time conveys an impression of coldness, meanness and lack of generosity in love.

'I am ... the captain of my soul' these are the last lines of a poem called 'Invictus', by a minor English poet W E Henley (1849–1903). Henley's poems are almost all about heroes, power and patriotism; 'Invictus' is a celebration of a man's power to conquer all hardships by sheer strength of will.

'Goodbye and keep cold' the title of a poem by Robert Frost (1875–1963), a great American poet who wrote a number of poems about the relationships between people, nature and God. In this poem he is talking about an orchard before the winter frosts set in (which are beneficial to the orchard) and saying that he cannot protect it, 'But something has to be left to God'.

108 *this ultimate violation* this final terrible act of destruction.

you are the King of Swords the man she has chosen treats her just as 'Aunt B' did. By naming him, she is reducing his power over her, and by recognising her own pattern of choice she is empowering herself to change the pattern.

Bella Makes Life

109 *Norman Manley Airport*   the airport of Kingston, Jamaica.

a checker cab   the yellow and black chequered cabs in
New York.

Bella no done yet   that wasn't all that was awful about her.

dyed her hair ... like it grease and spray   Bella has bleached
her black hair red, straightened it and then curled it, using a
special kit known as a Jherri curls kit.

Joseph never ever bother take in   Joseph didn't even notice.

DV   (Latin) Deo volente (God willing); here it means 'without fail'.

The lady who sponsor me   a system for controlling immigration
in which a prospective immigrant to the USA had to have a
sponsor who would be responsible for her/him in law.

to work some dollars ... to make life when I come home   it is
easier for immigrant women to find employment in the USA
than men. Notice the title of the story.

110 *laugh after him because is like him done with woman*
Joseph's friends laugh at him because he doesn't seem inter-
ested in women any more.

111 *Blerd Naught, a Bella dat, whatta way she favour checker
cab*   good Lord, is that Bella? She looks like a chequered cab!

'nuff'   inclined to do everything to extremes.

Bwoy, Bella a you broader than Broadway   you're very fat.

112 *Beverley Hills*   a residential area of Kingston in the hills above
the town, where the newly rich live.

is what happen to Bella?   but what had happened to Bella?

You no think say ... reason bout somethings?   do you think
you could stop the sales for a while so that you and I can have a
talk?

113 *you live well yah*   you're doing well from the sales, aren't you?

good breads   a lot of money.

A wha it so?   what does 'it' mean?

mine she want tie you   Peaches is suggesting that Miss Blossom might have used obeah (magic or supernatural powers) and put something in the food which would make Joe fall in love with her.

114 **Box feeding outta hog mouth**   steal food from the pigs in order to survive.

115 **anything stay too long will serve two masters**   if you dither you will lose what you have.

mi baby mother   the mother of my children.

Miami Vice   a television programme set in Miami: the female detective wore very bright floral clothing.

Bees mus take up Bella ... water her   bees must be deceived into trying to settle on Bella when she's wearing those flowery clothes. If she passes Hope Gardens (the national botanical gardens in Kingston) they'll mistake her for a plant and try to water her.

116 **posse**   friends (black American slang, which now has a considerable influence on Jamaican Creole vocabulary).

take time with that jagging suit   be careful with that jogging suit.

him son and him daughter heads well Jherri curls off   his son's and daughter's heads had been treated with the Jherri curls kit.

fi tun pimp   to turn into a pimp.

me ago black up you eye   I'll give you a black eye.

youth man   son

two by four   very small house.

117 **catch her fraid**   was scared.

make a check by Miss Blossom   visited Miss Blossom.

Fort Lawdadale   Fort Lauderdale.

draw a gear   change gear.

rasta man   Rastafarian, member of a religious group popular in Jamaica.

Study programme

Stories by Maya Angelou

Incident in the Yard

1 'Whatever the contest had been out front, I knew Momma had won.' What was the incident in the yard all about? Why was it a contest and how did Momma win it?

- Before you write about this, use your reading log and the questions below to discuss the incident in small groups, or you may prefer to put Momma in the 'hot seat' and let her answer questions about what happened.

- If you decide to 'hot-seat' Momma, choose someone to play the part of Momma and have her/him sit in front of the class or group and explain Momma's feelings and her actions. This person may need to have some advisers to help her/him. In groups, think of questions you could ask Momma. Use the questions below and look back on your notes about Mommas's changes of feelings and her 'body language' to get more ideas about what you could ask Momma.

  - What happened at the beginning of the story? Why does that matter?
  - What did Momma expect when she saw the powhitetrash children coming and what actually happened?
  - What did Maya not understand? How did Maya react?
  - Why did Maya Angelou say that 'something had happened out there' and later call it a contest?
  - What did Momma and Maya do after the incident and why does that matter?

Names

2 The structure of the story

Work with a partner or group and discuss the following questions. Now that you know the end, you are going to look for the ways that Maya Angelou builds towards the dramatic climax.

- What is the climax? Why does it please the reader?
- What information is given in the story that helps make the climax work so well at the end? Reread the story together, looking for clues.

  - Think of the historical and social context: how does the information that Maya Angelou gives us help us to understand the climax of the story?
  - What do we know of Maya's feelings towards Mrs Cullinan and how they change?
  - What else do we know of Maya's character?
  - How do we learn about the things that Mrs Cullinan values?
  - How does the renaming incident change Maya's behaviour?

- Look carefully at the way that Maya carries out her revenge. What exactly does she do? How does she add an extra touch to her revenge?
- How did you feel at the end of the story? What do you think Maya Angelou wanted to show in this story? Do you think she succeeded?

Now write an essay with this title: 'Maya Angelou carefully constructs her story so that all the elements are brought together in a satisfying climax'.

3 Irony

The term 'irony' is used in literature when the meaning you are intended to understand is the opposite of what is being said or done.

- At the beginning of the story, Maya Angelou says that a white lady who would 'quickly describe herself a liberal' calls her a debutante. What is ironic about these lines?

- What other examples of irony can you find in this story?

- Is the whole story an ironic play on the idea of a 'finishing school' (a school where debutantes and young ladies from wealthy families went to learn languages and how to behave in society)? If so, why?

Visit to the Dentist

4 Language

Look carefully at the language of the following passages:

- from the beginning of the story to 'She said he owed her a favor' (page 17);

- from 'He opened the door and looked at Momma' (page 19) to 'He turned his back and went through the door into the cool beyond' (page 20);

- the passage in italics (pages 20–1);

- Momma's version (page 23).

For each passage, discuss the vocabulary, dialect, length of sentences, tone (is it funny, ironic, threatening?), the speaker/narrator and the audience. Does awareness of the audience affect the language of the passage?

5 Parody

Maya's fantasy can be traced to the influence of film and comics (not television in the 1930s–1940s). It is almost a parody; that is, a humorous imitation of something, which makes fun of it by exaggerating certain characteristics. What is being parodied here is a certain type of film where the hero always puts every-thing right and the bad guy is made to pay.

Write about the way that Maya Angelou mixes humour with serious comment on society in this story.

Write a parody of something familar, such as a visit to the shops or something that happens at school (a lesson, assembly) in the style of a western, or a gangster film or a romance. Each type of film has its own vocabulary and style of action. You may want to read Roger McGough's poem 'The Lesson', which is a parody of discipline in an unruly classroom, or the short story 'The Secret Life of Walter Mitty' about a man who escapes from his troubles through fantasy.

Stories by Alice Walker

Nineteen Fifty-Five

☐ The structure of the story

This story is told chronologically, but it is episodic. Although it covers about twenty-five years, we only know of a few specific incidents relating to the relationship between Traynor and Gracie Mae.

Why do you think she included the incidents that she did – what is the connection between them?

How do we get a sense of time passing during the story? Which bits seem to 'go slower' or 'go faster'? Why might this be?

- Make a time-line of the events of the story. What choices do you think Alice Walker had to make about what to leave out?

- Think of some of the incidents that have been left out, or briefly referred to – such as J.T.'s death or Traynor's marriage. Choose an incident that has been left out and write an entry for it.

- Alice Walker tells her story through diary, present tense narrative, past tense narrative, letters, dialogue. Why does she vary the forms so much? What does this add to the story? Look at the beginning of the story and at the episodes of the visit to Traynor's house and to the Johnny Carson show: what does Alice Walker gain from using the present tense in these places?

- What is the effect on the reader of the way that Alice Walker has written her story? Write an essay on the structure of the story.

The Flowers

2 Language

Reread the story carefully looking for these particular features of Alice Walker's style and language:

- short dramatic sentences;
- similar patterns or rhythms in the sentences;
- two or more adjectives for the same noun;
- alliteration.

Find examples of these. What do they add to the mood of the story?

3 Symbolism

Alice Walker uses symbolism in this story: she uses one thing to represent and remind us of something else. The natural environment, the flowers Myop gathers and puts down, the rose growing through the noose, the noose itself and the remains on the tree are all symbolic.

- What does each of these symbolise?

- How has Alice Walker used them in the story to give additional levels of meaning that are never openly stated?
- Discuss why you think Alice Walker called this story '**The Flowers**'.

Write a critical appreciation of this story, using your work on language and symbolism.

To Hell with Dying

4 The relationship between Mr Sweet and the author

Alice Walker focuses our attention on Mr Sweet's appearance and personality: both of these obviously affected the children very much. Alice Walker says, in the last sentence of the story, that 'the man ... with ... the flowing white beard had been my first love'.

- Why do the children like Mr Sweet so much?
- What is significant about his appearance?
- What effect did Mr Sweet have on Alice Walker as she grew up?

Write an essay on Mr Sweet and the impact he had on Alice Walker's life.

5 Dealing with death

'... we had not learned that death was final when it did come' (page 49).

What was the children's attitude to death? How were they prepared for Mr Sweet's death?

Many young people have already had to deal with the death of someone they have loved. In a small group, or as a class, have a discussion about death and how young people should be prepared for it. You will need to be sensitive to each others' feelings. If you think you have some useful ideas about how parents and teachers could help young people to cope with death, discuss how you could share these ideas, perhaps through a class anthology or an open letter to the local paper.

6 Objects with special significance

In this story, Alice Walker draws our attention to the quilt cover and to the guitar. Both of these have a special significance for the author, because they bring back particular memories of Mr Sweet.

Write a short description of an object that you care deeply about. Describe its appearance and say what it means to you and why.

Stories by Olive Senior

Love Orange

1 Themes

Although it is short, this is a complex story and it works at a number of different levels. On one level, it tells about an imaginative child's fantasies but, on another level, it is about a child's need to be loved, about loneliness, about how children come to understand death and about the alienation of the child in the adult world.

Write an essay about the way that Olive Senior depicts childhood in '**Love Orange**'. Refer closely to the story.

2 Relationships in the story

The girl and her grandparents care for each other but they have difficulty showing their feelings.

* Work in a small group and make a tableau, by putting each

person into positions that you think represent the relation-ships in the story. Discuss why you have placed people as you have. Then look at another group's tableau. Is it different?

- What evidence is there that the girl and her grandparents love each other?

- What do we learn from the way the girl describes what she does at home and what happens when they go out? Why do you think the girl and her grandparents cannot understand each other?

Write a letter from the grandmother to the girl explaining how she feels about her and/or write the girl's reply. If you include information which is not in the story, make sure that it fits in with what we do know from the story about the girl's past.

3 Symbolism

A symbol is something real that represents something abstract like an idea or a feeling. There are a number of symbols in the story, of which the doll and the orange are the most obvious. Discuss these questions with a partner, or in a small group:

- The doll
  Share your ideas about the doll. Why was the doll so impor-tant to the girl? Why does it make her feel sick? Why does she bury it? How does it 'rise up one more time' as the grandmother is dying? When you think you have answered these questions, try to decide what the doll symbolises.

- The orange
  Why does the girl think of love as an orange? What does the way she sees love tell us about her experience of being loved? Why does she not dare to part with the love-orange even when she wants to give it to her grandmother or the dog? Why does she only feel safe giving it to dead or dying people?

- The ball, the shoebox, the talisman
  What do these symbols represent?

Write an essay about how Olive Senior uses symbols in the story to convey different levels of meaning.

Do Angels Wear Brassieres?

4 Write a critical appreciation of the episode with the Archdeacon.

To write a critical appreciation, you have to know what makes a text work well. You will find this easiest if you work in a small group for the discussion, although the reading and writing you will do on your own.

- Reread the text from 'Auntie Mary is a nervous wreck' (page 64) to 'throw kitchen cloth over her head and sit there bawling and bawling in sympathy' (page 68).

- How does Olive Senior build up to the moment when Auntie Mary opens the door and hears Beccka's question about the angels? Discuss how she uses the following features:
  - the humour;
  - the build up of tension;
  - the contrasts;
  - the expectation of the reader that disaster will strike;
  - the knowledge of the characters involved;
  - the pace of events;
  - the language;
  - the social context;
  - the irony.

- Use your reading log notes to help you. For example, you might notice that the pace of events goes fast in the preparations, slower as Auntie Mary prays Beccka will vanish, slower still as all seems to be well at the beginning of the visit, gets faster as the Archdeacon and Beccka tell jokes, slows down when they get to the 'serious questions' and speeds up dramatically when all becomes chaos. How does Olive Senior make it faster and slower? Look at the length of sentences and whether they are complete statements or whether they all rush into one another. Look at the liveliness of the language, especially the verbs (bounce, spill, hit, jump, throw way ...)

- Discuss each of the areas you thought were important and make some notes to help you write your essay. When you come to write your essay, organise your notes so that your writing goes smoothly from one topic into another and shows how Olive Senior has crafted the piece so that it works really well.

5 Write a character study of Beccka using your reading log notes and evidence from the text.

The Boy Who Loved Ice Cream

6 Work in a small group. Which of the following statements do you agree with? First go through the list and put a tick (√), a cross (x) or a question mark (?) against each one, according to whether you agree, disagree or don't know. Then compare and discuss your ideas, as a group.

1 Benjy's father hates the boy because he thinks Benjy is not his son.
2 Benjy's father is too possessive.
3 Benjy is not like his father.
4 Benjy's mother likes lots of people.
5 Benjy's father feels inadequate and blames other people for this.
6 Benjy's father is jealous of his wife.
7 Benjy is insecure.
8 Benjy's father is a kind man.
9 Benjy's mother is too frivolous,

10 Benjy's mother loves his father.
11 If the marriage breaks up it will be Benjy's mother's fault.
12 Benjy is the son of the townman.

When you discuss these statements, use evidence from the text to support your views. Do you think that Benjy's mother had had an affair with the townman in the purple shirt?

7 Expectations and disappointments

Each of the four in the family – Benjy, his father (Mr Seeter), his mother (Miss Mae) and his sister, Elsa – went to the fair with hopes and expectations. To what extent were these fulfilled or disappointed?

- Write a paragraph or two on each of the four members of the family showing how their hopes were fulfilled or not.

- Write a story on 'The biggest disappointment of my life' showing the anticipation, and the extent of the disappointment.

8 Alternative endings

Olive Senior stops the story at the high point of confusion. The conflict is not resolved: we do not know what happened next or what the result of the confrontation was for all those involved.

- Write the end of the story – you do not have to write it in the same 'stream of consciousness' style of the last part of the story.

- Write the story as a report in the *Trelawny Gazette*, the local newspaper. You will need to describe the events, and have an 'angle' on the story – interviews with 'neighbours' from the village or an interview with one of the main protagonists (perhaps with the townman in the purple shirt). You will need a headline and subheadings for the story.

Stories by Lorna Goodison

The Dolly Funeral

1 Groups of friends/gangs

If you were ever part of a gang or group of friends who did things together, who was the leader? Why? How was the rest of the hierarchy (order of importance) decided?

Think about leadership:

- What qualities does a leader need?
- Was Bev a good leader? Why?
- Was the leader of your group a good leader? Why?
- Did the leadership ever change? Why?

Think about the activities of the group in the story:

- Have you ever disobeyed your parents/guardians to join a group of friends doing something the adults did not approve of?
- Did you get into trouble? Did you regret it later or were you glad to have done it anyway?
- If you had been in Bev's group, would you have tried to prevent them from teasing Rowena? How? Have you ever tried to persuade your friends not to do something?

Write a story about the activity of a gang or group of friends, using some of the ideas you have thought about or discussed above.

I Come Through

2 The title 'I come through'

The story starts with the singer's success with a song, the last line of which is the title of the story. Like many of Lorna Goodison's stories, this one fuses the physical and the spiritual.

The singer finds the strength to overcome her difficulties and to 'come through' in different ways and from different sources.

Think about these questions:

- What difficulties did the singer have to overcome?
- In what way did her children give her strength?
- What did she learn from the dream?
- What inner strength did she find within herself?

I Don't Want to Go Home in the Dark

3 Symbolism

This story rewards careful discussion, although there are sometimes no 'right' answers. Discuss the symbolism in the story:

- How is the man's materialism symbolised in the story?
- What did the woman's leaving her body mean?
- How does money come into the story?
- Why are the pregnant cat and the azaleas special?
- What is she looking for when she looks for some spare love or a 'kiss left languidly on a smooth surface' (page 101)?
- What do candles with drips represent that is different from 'clean' candles?
- Why does she ask for azaleas?
- What is significant about the music?
- Why does she want to bathe with a soap called Wild Flowers?

Much of this story is fantasy; it relates also to the Caribbean folk figure of 'Ol' Hige', a witch, who slips out of her skin at night to suck the blood of young children and babies. There are ways of stopping the Ol' Hige getting back into her skin, by putting salt and pepper on it and saying the right words.

4 Characters in the story

The woman

- Write a description of the woman. What do we know about her? What is important to her?
- You may enjoy Lorna Goodison's poems '**Mulatta Song (II)**' and '**Farewell to Wild Woman (II)**'. Both of them have a strong relationship with this story.

The man

- Write a description of the man. Start with a paragraph about the man's appearance and then write two or three paragraphs about his character as shown in his behaviour and his words.
- Imagine the man is giving an account of the evening to a friend over dinner: what do you think he would have said? Write this either as a dialogue or as a monologue (that is, as if the man was saying it). Don't change the events of the story, but present them as the man would have seen them.

Write an essay comparing and contrasting the characters of the man and the woman.

The King of Swords

5 The abuse of power

Work in a small group to discuss these questions:

- In what ways do (a) 'Aunt B' and (b) the man bully the narrator?
- What effect does this have on her opinion of herself?
- Does the narrator contribute to her own bullying by becoming a 'victim'? How does she change this?
- Why does she call the aunt an 'old hige'?

- Why do you think the narrator chooses a man like this to love?

The woman finds a way to stop being bullied and to empower herself.

- How does she do this?
- Do you think it will work?

Use these ideas as the basis for an essay called: 'Issues of power in "**The King of Swords**"'.

6 Imaginatively developing the story

The story says that the aunt 'had been very beautiful in her time' (page 105). When the aunt dies after a long illness, her journal is found. In it she has written about her own life, her feelings about the girl and why she behaved as she did. Write three entries from the journal. They can be from any point in the aunt's life, but should relate to the story.

Bella Makes Life

7 The letters

The three letters in the story are very important; each one of them takes the story forward a stage and tells us something about the relationship between Bella and Joe Joe. Write three letters from Joe Joe to Bella:

- one letter in response to Bella's first letter;
- the one he wrote after Peaches had told Joe Joe she had seen Bella;
- one after Bella's third letter.

8 Male and female roles

An underlying theme in this story is what Bella and Joe Joe think the roles of men and women are. Bella says Joe Joe is 'behind time' and must 'come forward' because this is 'the age of women's liberation'. Work in small groups and discuss these questions about men's and women's roles. If you are in a mixed class you may find it interesting to have some boys only groups, some girls only and some mixed pairs or groups.

- What do you think traditional male and female roles are?
- Do you think Bella is fair in saying Joe Joe is 'behind time'?
- In what ways do Bella and Joe Joe take traditional roles and in what ways are they different?
- Do you think there are traditional roles for men and women in your culture or society now? What are these roles? Do you personally agree with them?

Share your ideas as a class discussion and then prepare a debate on the changing roles of men and women in Britain in the 1990s.

Study questions on the anthology

Many of the activities you have already completed will help you to answer the following questions. Before you begin to write, consider these points about essay writing:

- Think about what the question is asking. Underline key words or phrases.
- Use each part of the question to 'brainstorm' ideas and references to the stories which you think are relevant to the answer.
- Decide on the order in which you are going to tackle the parts of the question.
- Write a first draft of your essay.
- Redraft as many times as you need, ensuring all the time that:
  - each paragraph answers the question;

- you have an opening and closing paragraph which is clear and linked to the question set;
- you have checked for spelling and other grammatical errors.

1 Discuss one of the following themes in relation to at least two stories in this anthology.

- growing up away from your parents
- the happiness and unhappiness of childhood
- a 'sense of community'
- relationships between women and men
- dealing with racism
- the influence of religion
- journeys
- friendship

2 An underlying theme in this anthology is the power of women to survive and shape their own future, despite adversity. Explore this theme in any number of the stories.

3 Relationships between black and white people are part of the background to many of these stories. Choose two or three stories, then set them in a historical and social context and explain how, as works of literature, they relate to this context.

4 Explore the influence of the oral tradition on the language and style of two or more of the stories.

5 Music is important in many of these stories, in particular in '**Nineteen Fifty-Five**' and '**I Come Through**'. Trace the development and influence of black music in any way that interests you and present your findings to the class in a talk with music. You may have seen the film *The Harder They Come* which includes an interesting perspective on the music industry

in Jamaica and on exploitation of the singer, which echoes both the stories in this anthology.

6 Some of these stories involve the loss of innocence. Compare the loss of happiness in '**The Flowers**' and '**Love Orange**'.

7 Many of the stories reflect the experiences of children. Choose examples from the stories by Maya Angelou, '**To Hell with Dying**', '**The Dolly Funeral**' or the stories by Olive Senior to show how the writer reflects the experiences of children in the adult world, where rules are difficult to remember and adult behaviour is hard to understand.

Write an essay on the portrayal of children in the adult world by any two writers in this collection.

8 Discuss the relationships between children and adults in three or more stories. Consider the different expectations that adults and children have of each other and to what extent these are fulfilled. Choose at least one relationship which you consider satisfactory and one which you consider unsatisfactory and explain why this is so.

9 Some of the stories are concerned with young people dealing with death. Compare the impact of death on the children in '**The Flowers**', '**Love Orange**' and '**To Hell with Dying**'.

10 Discuss setting and its effect in three or more stories in this collection.

11 Explore what Alice Walker has called 'the richness of the black woman's experience' by comparing and contrasting the older women in the following stories:

- Grandmother Henderson (Momma) in any or all of Maya Angelou's stories

- Gracie Mae in '**Nineteen Fifty-Five**'
- The singer in '**I Come Through**'

12 To what extent do you think the writers in this collection have written the stories they wanted to read and have become their own role models, as Alice Walker said?

Suggestions for further reading

The stories, novels and poems listed below are almost all written by black women and relate to the themes of the stories in this anthology.

Maya Angelou

- *Incident in the Yard*

    '**Frankie Mae**' by Jean Wheeler Smith, from *Black-eyed Susans*, edited by Mary Helen Washington
    Words by Heart by Ouida Sebestyen

- *Names*

    '**Her true-true name**' by Merle Hodge, from *Her true-true name* edited by Pamela Mordecai and Betty Wilson
    '**A Name is Sometimes an Ancestor Saying Hi I'm With You**' by Alice Walker, from *Living by the Word*

- *Visit to the Dentist*

    Edith Jackson by Rosa Guy
    Underground to Canada by Barbara M Smucker

Alice Walker

- *Nineteen Fifty-Five*

  '**Rambler**' by Julius Lester, from ***Long Journey Home***

- *The Flowers*

  Roll of Thunder, Hear My Cry by Mildred D Taylor
  Let the Circle Be Unbroken by Mildred D Taylor

- *To Hell with Dying*

  '**The old artist: notes on Mr Sweet**' by Alice Walker, from
      Living by the Word
  The Friends by Rosa Guy

Olive Senior

- *Love Orange*

  Christopher by Geoffrey Drayton
  '**Summer Lightning**' by Olive Senior, from the anthology
      Summer Lightning

- *Do Angels Wear Brassieres?*

  Crick Crack, Monkey by Merle Hodge

- *The Boy Who Loved Ice Cream*

  Beka Lamb, by Zee Edgell

Lorna Goodison

- *The Dolly Funeral*

  Whole of a Morning Sky by Grace Nichols

- *I Come Through*

  '**From the poets in the kitchen**' by Paule Marshall, from ***Merle and other stories***

- *I Don't Want to go Home in the Dark*

  Annie John by Jamaica Kincaid

- *The King of Swords*

  Wide Sargasso Sea by Jean Rhys

- *Bella Makes Life*

  Jamaica Labrish by Louise Bennett (Sangsters Book Stores, Kingston, Jamaica)

Wider reading assignments

1. Compare and contrast the way that characters deal with racism in the rural Southern states presented in '**Frankie Mae**', ***Words by Heart*** and '**Incident in the Yard**' and '**The Flowers**' or in the novels of Mildred D Taylor.

2. Many of these stories are of resistance and courage in the face of adversity. Explore this theme through the novels of Rosa Guy and Barbara M Smucker and relate it to any stories in this anthology.

3. Class issues in the Caribbean emerge in a number of novels and stories. Discuss the presentation of class issues in the stories of Olive Senior or Lorna Goodison and compare this with one or more of the following novels: ***Christopher***, ***Crick Crack, Monkey***, ***Beka Lamb*** or ***Whole of a Morning Sky***.

4. Compare the short-story writing of any of the writers in this

anthology with their non-fiction prose or poetry. To what extent do the same themes emerge in the fiction and non-fiction (prose or poetry) of your chosen writer? Do you find the fiction or non-fiction more effective?

5 Which of the writers you have read speaks with the strongest voice for women? Explain your answer.

Addison Wesley Longman Limited,
Edinburgh Gate, Burnt Mill, Harlow,
Essex CM20 2JE, England
and Associated Companies throughout the world.

This educational edition first published 1996

Editorial material set in 10/12 point Gill Sans
Produced by Longman Singapore Publishers (Pte) Ltd
Printed in Singapore

ISBN 0 582 28730 8

Cover illustration by Hamish Blakely

The publisher's policy is to use paper manufactured from
sustainable forests.

Consultant: *Geoff Barton*

Acknowledgements
We are grateful to the following for permission to reproduce copyright material:
Maya Angelou for 'Incident in the Yard', 'Names', and 'Visit to the Dentist' from *I
Know Why the Caged Bird Sings* (published by Virago Press Ltd 1990) © Maya
Angelou 1969; Lorna Goodison for her stories 'The Dolly Funeral', 'I Come
Through' and 'I Don't Want to Go Home in the Dark' from *Baby Mother and the
King of Swords* © Longman Group UK Ltd (1990); Olive Senior for her stories 'Love
Orange', 'Do Angels Wear Brassieres?' and 'The Boy Who Loved Icecream' from
Summer Lightning and Other Stories © Longman Group UK Ltd 1989; Alice Walker
for her stories 'Nineteen Fifty-Five' © 1981 by Alice Walker, 'The Flowers' © 1969
by Alice Walker, and 'To Hell with Dying' © 1967 by Alice Walker.

Longman Literature
Series editor: Roy Blatchford

Plays

Alan Ayckbourn   *Absurd Person Singular*   0 582 06020 6
Ad de Bont   *Mirad, A Boy from Bosnia*   0 582 24949 X
Oliver Goldsmith   *She Stoops to Conquer*   0 582 25397 7
Henrik Ibsen   *Three plays: The Wild Duck, Ghosts and
   A Doll's House*   0 582 24948 1
Ben Jonson   *Volpone*   0 582 25408 6
Christopher Marlowe   *Doctor Faustus*   0 582 25409 4
Arthur Miller   *An Enemy of the People*   0 582 09717 7
Terence Rattigan   *The Winslow Boy*   0 582 06019 2
Jack Rosenthal   *Wide-Eyed and Legless*   0 582 24950 3
Willy Russell   *Educating Rita*   0 582 06013 3
                    Shirley Valentine   0 582 08173 4
Peter Shaffer   *Equus*   0 582 09712 6
                    The Royal Hunt of the Sun   0 582 06014 1
Bernard Shaw   *Arms and the Man*   0 582 07785 0
                    The Devil's Disciple   0 582 25410 8
                    Pygmalion   0 582 06015 X
                    Saint Joan   0 582 07786 9
R B Sheridan   *The Rivals* and *The School for Scandal*   0 582 25396 9
J Webster   *The Duchess of Malfi*   0 582 28731 6
Oscar Wilde   *The Importance of Being Earnest*   0 582 07784 2

Longman Literature Shakespeare
Series editor: Roy Blatchford

Antony and Cleopatra   0 582 28727 8 (paper)
As You Like It   0 582 23661 4 (paper)
Coriolanus   0 582 28726 X
Hamlet   0 582 09720 7 (paper)
Henry IV Part 1   0 582 23660 6 (paper)
Henry V   0 582 22584 1 (paper)
Julius Caesar   0 582 08828 3 (paper)
                    0 582 24589 3 (cased)
King Lear   0 582 09718 5 (paper)
Macbeth   0 582 08827 5 (paper)
                    0 582 24592 3 (cased)
The Merchant of Venice   0 582 08835 6 (paper)
                    0 582 24593 1 (cased)
A Midsummer Night's Dream   0 582 08833 X (paper)
                    0 582 24590 7 (cased)
Othello   0 582 09719 3 (paper)
Richard III   0 582 23663 0 (paper)
Romeo and Juliet   0 582 08836 4 (paper)
                    0 582 24591 5 (cased)
The Tempest   0 582 22583 3 (paper)
Twelfth Night   0 582 08834 8 (paper)
The Winter's Tale   0 582 28728 6

Other titles in the Longman Literature series are listed on page ii.